Love

You

Most

(Book 2 of the *Hate To Love* duet)

Also by Alexis Bice

This Love Is Ours

Life Unlocked

Don't You Dare

Hate You More (Book 1 of the Hate To Love duet)

"I am the book and the book is me. Words flow through my veins like blood. I need them to survive. It's my oxygen. My lifeline. My escape from a world that can be so dark and so scary, that sometimes I need to just get away for a little while and live the life of someone else."

-Alexis Bice

LOVE YOU MOST

Acknowledgments

Thank you, thank you, thank you to all of my readers and supporters. YOUR support means the absolute world to me! I am entirely grateful to have even a few hours of your life dedicated to reading my stories.

Amanda Alger Rice: Thank you SO much for being my editor and for all of your feedback. You never let me down, and the hours upon hours you spend working on my books mean more to me than you will ever know. I am so lucky to have you with me on this journey!

Hype Girls

Melissa Baxter: Even with all that you have going on, you still read and promote all of my books. You are truly a BADASS. I hope for the very best for you because you DESERVE IT.

Kelsie Britton: From my very first book and your support at my book signing, you have been so great to me. Thank you, thank you, thank you!!!

Chantel Curry: For someone I have never met in person, you have been such an angel. You're always so eager to help and post about my books and your kind words and excitement mean so much to me. Not a single post goes unnoticed, and I thank you from the bottom of my heart!

Sarah Evans: You are one of the kindest souls I have ever met. You never fail at making me feel good, and your support is endless. Thank you so much!

LOVE YOU MOST

Chelsea Fox: I LOVE your excitement. It is contagious. Your support means everything to me. Thank you!

Makayla Garnsey: You're always so eager to get my books in your hands and I appreciate you so much! You're just the best. I love you my Dizzle!

Jessica Gentry: Jessica, you have been such a big help to me, and I thank you so much for all that you do!

Shirley Hellinger: Girl, you are always so excited and eager to help hype up my books and read them. I am so lucky to have you, and I could never thank you enough!

Journey Hoffert: Having your support has been such a blessing to me. You have been such a big supporter since my very first book, and I am so grateful to have you on my side.

Charlene Johnson: Thank you SO much for all of your help. You seriously rock.

JoEllen LaFontaine: You have been such an angel. Your kind words have lifted me up more than you know at times when I need it the most. Thank you for being you!

Lisa: I LOVE that you are so raw and honest. Your feedback means so much to me and I thank you so much for that. Your honest feedback will only help me grow as a writer. Thank you.

Danielle Makuch: Thank you for all of your help in promoting my books! You are always so kind and supportive.

Megan: Ever since you found out I was publishing my first book, you have always been so excited for me, and your feedback and help means the world to me. You are *awesome.*

Lexi Moser: You are so good to me! Your excitement of my books makes me feel SO good, and I am so grateful to have you on my team!

Brittany Teal: I am SO excited to have you on my side! You've always been such an awesome supporter since day one!

Randi-Lynn Ward Singleton: You have always been so helpful in getting the word of my books out, and I cannot possibly thank you enough!!!

Dedication

I'd like to dedicate this book to my biggest fan, my
Grandma. You're always so excited and counting down the
days to my new release, and you read and support me like
no other. Having your support means the world to me, and I
am so thankful to have you on my side, cheering me on.
My love for reading undoubtedly stems from you. As a
little girl, I would always come to your house and spend
time in my bedroom reading and writing. You've given me
countless books to read over the years and I am so happy to
finally be able to give them back to you. I love you with all
my heart.

XoXo,
Bunzy

They say there's a thin line between love and hate. Little did I know, I'd find out just how true that statement was...

Prologue

Greyson

Then: Nineteen years old

I woke to the sound of the baby crying, or was that the doorbell? Fuck, it was too early for this. I lifted my head, and peered over at the clock – 6:04, too damn early for a Saturday. I looked over to my wife who was lying next to me still sound asleep. I hoped today would be a better day. No fighting. No bickering. No yelling. One could hope right?

I heard a dinging come from downstairs, and I knew that it must have been the doorbell that sounded the first time.

I rose from the bed, and groggily rubbed my eyes. As I passed by Lennon's room, I saw that she was still sleeping soundly. A smile tugged at my lips as I admired her dark curls, looking so much like her mother when she sleeps.

The doorbell rang again, and I groaned.

"I'm coming!" *Christ, who the hell would be ringing somebody's doorbell at six-o-fucking-clock in the morning on a Saturday?*

I opened the door, and stood face-to-face with a man I didn't recognize. He was dressed in stained up jeans and a leather jacket. I noticed an impressive looking Harley parked on the side of the road, and my heart fell to the pit of my stomach.

I bore my eyes into a pair of icy blues, and for a second, I thought I was looking into a mirror.

"Hello, Son."

Chapter One

Vaeda

Then: Eighteen years old

It was the happiest day of my life, or it was supposed to be anyway. Today was the day I was marryin' the love of my life, or so I thought. Maybe he was the love of my life. Maybe things weren't always a fairytale in real life like they were in the books and movies. I just thought it would have been different than this. Gettin' married at the courthouse with only a drunken Liam by our side. It took a hell of a lot of convincin' on Greyson's part to even get him here, but we needed a witness. Our families weren't very acceptin' of our spur of the moment shotgun weddin'. Mine more than his. It didn't matter anyway. Lennon was supposed to be here. My parents were supposed to be here. I was supposed to feel happier than I did. I looked down to the basketball-sized bulge that was my belly, and wrapped my arms around it. I was doin' this for her. She deserves a family. A mama and a daddy who loved each other no matter how much it hurt.

I haven't always been fair to you. I know that. But that's how we communicated. Bully. Fight. Hate. Love. It's what we did. But we were kids, Vaeda. And I need you to know that I would never take your love for granted. Greyson's words rang loud in my ears as I wiped away a fallen tear from my cheek. Never take my love for granted? Oh, right. That's why I found dick pics on your phone that sure as hell weren't sent to me.

I took a deep breath in, and joined my soon-to-be husband at the altar. To make vows to the man who continued to break my heart day after day, hopin' and prayin' that one day things would be different. *For her.*

Chapter Two

Greyson

Then: Nineteen years old

It wasn't much of a wedding, but what do you expect with no money and no family to support you? Our baby was due to be born any day now, and I was adamant that I wanted to be married before she arrived. Vaeda's Aunt Dot and Uncle Henry were still pissed. More Henry than Dotty. They'd accused me of sabotaging Vaeda's medical career by intentionally getting her pregnant. *Right.* As if I fucking wanted this? I had a whole career ahead of me. I still do. Nothing was going to change that. I lived for football. I lived for everyone's eyes to be on me, watching and cheering me on. There was no greater feeling in the world. Vaeda was still going to be a doctor. Things just happened a little out of order. But that's okay. I was still going to Ohio State, as much as Vaeda hated it. She hated

15

being apart. She was still going to school back home, and thankfully, freshman year was over. Long distance was definitely hard on our relationship, but it had to be done for now. I needed the distance. I still came home on breaks and for the summer, and we FaceTimed most days. When Vaeda would answer, that is.

I couldn't help but feel uneasy as we walked out of the courthouse. I could see the tears brimming in Vaeda's eyes the entire ceremony, and her "I do" couldn't have sounded less sincere if she were marrying a frog. Even the kiss felt meaningless, and nothing Vaeda and I did together had ever felt like that before. Her touch always sent an electric shock through my veins and set my skin on fire. But now, all I felt was anger. Hurt. Betrayed. Unwanted. Unloved. I wanted to go back and pinpoint where everything had gone so very wrong, but then a part of me already knew. And a part of me just didn't give a damn. She was my wife now. We were days away from having a daughter. We were going to be a happy family, whether either of us liked it or not.

Chapter Three

Vaeda

Present day

I felt so dang proud as I walked across the stage, and held my diploma in my hands. I'd waited eight long years for this, but really my entire life. I'd always known I wanted to be a surgeon. I'd never wanted to be anythin' else. Things were finally comin' together.

I heaved a sigh of relief, as I walked off stage and into the arms of my daughter.

"Is it time for my birthday party now? That was seriously longer than *The Titanic*, Mom," Lennon said, makin' us all laugh.

"Yes, we can go have your birthday party now." I ran my hand through her jet-black curls, and smiled at how grown up she looked today in her white sundress than matched my own, with little blue flowers embroidered along the hem.

"Eight years old and already callin' the shots," Uncle Henry said, pullin' me in for a tight hug. "I'm so dang proud of you, Kiddo. You've done a hell of a job, and I know you'll make a great doctor. Soon enough you'll be makin' enough money to retire your old uncle," he said with a wink.

"Yeah, yeah. Thanks, Uncle Henry," I laughed.

"Is you-know-who gonna be at the party?" he asked, forcin' me to swallow the giant lump hoverin' in the back of my throat. *Who the hell knows?*

"Ya never know with him." Greyson and I were currently on a trial separation, and the more time that passed, the more I just wanted a divorce and to put that whole part of my life behind me. It had never been a true marriage, he'd never been faithful, and we'd never been a *real* family. I spent years wallowin' in self-pity, and tryin' to make up for all of my shortcomings, but it was never enough. No matter how hard I tried, I would never be enough for Greyson Tucker. Not that I ever was to begin

18

with. So I stopped tryin' and I started puttin' myself first for once.

"Mama, can we stop and see Aunt Dot before the party?" Lennon asked on the car ride home. I watched Uncle Henry look at her through the rearview mirror, and I could see the gloss flash across his older deep-green eyes. It was quick, but it was there.

"I don't think we'll have time to, Sweetheart. Not today," I replied in an even tone.

"We can stop in for thirty minutes or so. I'm sure she'd love to see her," Uncle Henry said, soundin' braver than he looked.

As we pulled in to the Gator Hill Residential Facility, my stomach knotted up, and I had to take a couple deep breaths so that I didn't pass out. The three of us trotted inside together, with Lennon in the middle, holdin' each of our hands.

After we checked in at the front desk, I knocked on Dotty's door.

"Dotty? It's Vaeda, Uncle Henry, and Lennon. May we come in?" Nothin'. "Dotty?" I called again, knockin' once more.

A minute later the door opened, and Dotty's roommate, Stella, answered the door, lookin' as pretty as ever in her lavender slacks and matchin' sweater.

"Hi, Stella. Is Dotty awake?" I asked, happy to see her. Stella was a good twenty-five years older than Dotty, but their condition was the same. She was a retired surgeon from the same hospital I'd be startin' my internship at next month. *Small world.*

"Oh, Vaeda! Why, yes, come in." Stella opened the door wider for us, and the three of us walked into the room, and found Dotty knittin' in her rockin' chair.

"Did you just graduate today?" Stella asked, her eyes examinin' my cap and gown carefully. I'd left it on for Dotty to see.

"Medical school, actually. I'm startin' my internship next month at St. Paul's. I'm goin' to be a surgeon just like you were, Stella," I reminded her again.

20

"Oh. You're taking my place? I'm coming back after my maternity leave, you know," she said, waggin' a wrinkly, yet perfectly polished pointer finger at me.

"That's okay. I'll just hold your spot until you get back." I smiled at Stella, and noticed that Dotty was starin' straight at Lennon.

"Vaeda. You look pretty today." She was smilin' warmly at her, and my heart melted into a little puddle at my feet. Uncle Henry and I exchanged glances, and we both knew that today wasn't a good day for Dotty.

"Thanks," Lennon replied, goin' along with it. "Did you know today's my eighth birthday? We're having a party when we get home," Lennon said, matter-of-fact.

"Why yes, of course we are. Henry, did you wash off that old tarp? The kids can't be sliding all over that thing until it's washed." Dotty looked sternly at Uncle Henry, and his lips formed into a little half-smile.

"It's already done, my love." It took me a minute to understand, but once I caught on, I realized she thought it was *my* eighth birthday, and was rememberin' when all of us kids turned Uncle Henry's blue tarp into a slip'n slide.

21

She had a pretty good memory for someone who couldn't remember her own name half the time. Lennon just smiled at her and took a seat across the room in the other rockin' chair.

"I'm so proud of you, you know," Dotty said, lookin' right at me.

"You are?" I asked, taken my surprise. Her words caught my off guard, but they meant so much more than she would ever know.

"You've always wanted to be a surgeon since you were just a little girl. I never doubted that you would be. Even when you got pregnant at such a young age..." her voice faded off into the distance, and I closed my eyes, cherishin' the present moment with my aunt if only for a fleetin' moment. It was always hard for me to come and visit Dotty and to see her mind deteriorate right before my eyes. But I still made time to come on the weekends, usually when Lennon was at her dad's house. I didn't like to bring Lennon all the time because I was always worried she would get upset if Dotty didn't remember her. Uncle

Henry came to visit her every single day, religiously, for the past year and a half that she's been here.

At first, it was just small things that she'd forgotten. Different recipes that she'd known by heart for years, or to stop and grab milk or eggs when they were out, or where she put her keys. Then it escalated into bigger things like people's birthdays or payin' a bill. Uncle Henry finally urged her to see her doctor when he walked into the house after work one day, and she'd forgotten who he was. She started yellin', throwin' things, hittin' him, and tellin' him to get out of her house, and that her husband was gonna be home soon and would shoot him if he caught him there.

Her doctor confirmed my suspicions that she had early-onset dementia, and our hearts completely shattered. She was only fifty-eight at the time, and though I knew from medical school that it could happen at any age, it was so surreal that it was happenin' to one of my loved ones right before my face.

In the beginning, it was only every once in a while. But then it began to occur daily and interfere with her normal, everyday life. And at which point, Uncle Henry talked about sellin' the ranch to Uncle Reed, and stayin' home to take care of her, but he knew that money would only last so long. He had to work to make a livin', and although I knew it killed him to do so, he had to put her in a home. I know he still feels incredibly guilty about it, hence why he visits her every single day after work, but I knew it was the right choice.

I brought Uncle Henry take-out a lot from the diner where I worked, because I felt bad that Dotty wasn't there to cook. I was always so busy with Lennon and school that I rarely ever had time to cook, myself.

I let Uncle Henry and Dotty chat amongst themselves for a few minutes while she seemed to be in good spirits, and went over to sit with Lennon, who was hummin' away a new song she'd learned in school.

He still loved her with every ounce of his bein'. I admired their marriage so much that it made my heart crumble in my chest that I didn't have that. I always said I wanted a love like Uncle Henry and Dotty. Like Lennon and Liam…

"Shamus." I shook out of my thoughts, as Dotty started talkin'. "Oh, Shamus that's such a nice song. Sing more, Shamus." My stomach knotted into a giant ball. Lennon raised a curious eyebrow at me, but I just shook my head at her, signalin' to go along with it. Poor girl. This is why I didn't normally like to bring her with me. She was too young to understand the complexity of Dotty's illness, but I know how much she loved her great aunt and how much Dotty loved her in return.

After we left the residential facility, I could see Lennon lookin' at me through the side-view mirror from the back seat. When she saw me make eye contact, she cocked her head to the side, and asked what was on her mind.

"Mama, why did Aunt Dot call me Shamus? He's a boy." I took a sharp breath before answerin'.

"Because your Uncle Shamus loves to sing just like you, honey," I answered truthfully.

"Oh yeah, I remember. Meemaw said he's a famous country singer in Nashville. Can we go watch him in concert sometime, Mama?" she asked, her eyes lightin' up at the thought.

"We'll see, baby. Maybe some time."

"I asked Daddy to bring me, but he said it wasn't a good idea. But it's just *so cool* that I'm related to someone famous." I glanced at her once more in the side-view mirror, before turnin' up the radio, signalin' the end of the conversation. But when I did, of course none other than Shay Tucker's new hit single *Show Me*, started blarin' through the speakers, and I shut it off.

Chapter Four

Greyson

Present day

It was almost two o'clock, and I knew I was almost two hours late for Lennon's birthday party. I'd had a five and a half hour drive from Nashville, but I got held up in traffic of course. I should've left earlier to allow some extra travel time, but I had to hit the gym and get some conditioning done. I was four months away from starting my fifth season with the Tennessee Titans, and I noticed I was losing some of my bulk and drive, and as the star quarterback that could *not* happen.

As I pulled into the driveway of the house I bought but didn't live in, I noticed people were already headed to their cars and leaving. *Shit.*

"Daddyyyyyyy!" Lennon yelled, as she ran full force straight into my arms. I picked her up and spun her into a little circle, before planting a kiss onto the top of her head. *God, I've missed her.*

"Party's over, Greyson. You shoulda been here two hours ago." The hair on the back of my neck stood straight up, as the voice of my wife sent chills down my spine. Chills from the icy tone of her voice, and chills because I hadn't heard that voice in over a month. We'd texted here and there regarding Lennon only, and when I came to pick her up on the weekends, she'd sent her out on her own. It's like she was hiding from me.

"Vaeda, come on. You know I had a long drive. I should've left sooner. I'm sorry." She continued picking up the lawn that was strewn with unicorn birthday decorations, and ignored me completely.

"I got you something, Len. Do you wanna open it?" I asked excitedly, as I planted her feet back on the ground, and opened the back door of my silver Audi.

"I hope it's an easy bake oven!" she squealed, making my heart swell in my chest.

"Even better," I winked, and handed her the giant box that was pretty piss poorly wrapped. She dug into the pink paper, and screamed so loud I thought I'd have to get fitted for a hearing aid when I got back to Nashville.

"A new guitar?!?! Mommy, look it! Daddy got me a new guitar!" Vaeda stopped what she was doing, and pulled her lips into a tight line.

"That's great, Sweetie."

"Y'know, Greyson, money can't buy love," Vaeda said, as she bustled around the kitchen after I'd invited myself in. It was my house after all. I made the monthly mortgage payment and I hadn't even lived here in four years. That was half of Lennon's life.

"Money?" I scoffed. She was unbelievable. "It's a fucking guitar, Vaeda, not a Lamborghini."

"Yeah well, all I could afford to buy her was a new art set, which she told me she already has. So yeah, I feel like mother of the year right now. Excuse me if I'm a little hurt by you not communicatin' with me about the gift. Or you know, bein' two hours late to your daughter's birthday." *She can't be fucking serious right now.*

"You couldn't *afford* to buy her something? Tell me you're joking. You live in my house completely free of

29

expense, and last time I checked, we had a joint fucking bank account with six figures in there, thanks to me. And I already apologized for running late. It wasn't my fault."

"It wasn't your fault? Of course it was your fault!" she fumed, taking two long strides across the kitchen, and getting into my face. Good thing Lennon was swinging in the backyard, because this could get ugly.

"You already know I refuse to touch your money. We're not together, and I don't want it. I only use what I absolutely have to, and you know that. Once I start my new job, I won't need a goddamn penny from you, ya hear?"

When she got mad, she had such a southern twang about her, and it really fucking turned me on. I shouldn't be this hungry for someone who I couldn't stand, but what could I say? A man still has needs. I closed the space between us by standing up, and bringing my nose to hers.

"I want you to use every cent that you could ever want. You know why? Because you're my goddamn wife, Vaeda," I spoke in a low, gruff tone through clenched teeth.

"Yeah, not for long," she scoffed, backing away from me. I grabbed her by the arm and pulled her back closer to me, and she didn't fight it. Her breath was hot and sweet in my face. That familiar vanilla and peach scent practically burned through my nose and set my skin on fire. My cock jolted upright in my jeans, and I'd be surprised if she didn't feel me poking her tight belly. She cocked her head to the side and let her breath warm my earlobe. I groaned at the feel of having a woman so damn close to me. So close I could taste it. *Taste her.*

"Greyson?" she whispered softly, making my insides boil with desire, as I shut my eyes, and soaked in the moment.

"The day I divorce your ass, will be the best day of my fuckin' life." And she walked away. Just like that. Her words ringing through my ears and cutting me in half.

Chapter Five

Greyson

Then: Nineteen years old

"Hello, Greyson," the man in front of me said, as the smoke from his Marlboro rolled out of his nose. Even his voice sounded just like mine, though older and raspier. Probably from many years of smoking, if I were to guess.

"Colt?" I asked, although I already knew the answer. His dirty-blonde hair was shoulder length and straggly from his bike ride, or not being washed in days, or maybe both. His face was scruffy with sand-colored facial hair, and he ran his other hand through his beard, as if he were lost in thought. His blue eyes locked with mine, and it pained me to look at them. Eyes that have surely seen some fucked up shit. Eyes that have caused so much pain and been in so much pain. He chuckled softly, as he took one last drag of his cigarette, before stomping it out on my steps.

"I think you mean *Dad*?" he asked, his eyes dancing with amusement.

"You're not my dad. I don't even know you. What the fuck are you even doing here?" I asked, wondering if I was still asleep. Maybe this was just a dream. It made no sense.

"I came to meet you," he said, seriously. "Fuck…you look just fuckin' like me." He chuckled again, looking away and shaking his head with disbelief. "Your ma was a hoe back in the day, but I guess you really are mine, huh?" he said more to himself than to me.

"You showed up at my house at six o'clock in the morning to *meet me*?" He shrugged his shoulders as if it were no big deal. Biological father showing up on his son's doorstep at six in the morning after nineteen years of not knowing him. Never trying to know him. Never giving a damn.

"What's goin' on?" Vaeda asked, peeking her chin over my shoulder. *Motherfucker.* Of course, the woman who could easily sleep in until eleven, would choose today of all days to be an early bird. She crossed her arms over her chest, hugging her champagne colored robe to her small figure. Her hair hung in loose waves all around her shoulders, and she looked like she was still half asleep. Until she looked from me to Colt, and then back at me. Clearly she must have noticed the shocking resemblance, because her eyes were certainly wide and alert now. No coffee even needed.

"Is that…"

"*Holy shit*," Colt spoke, not taking his eyes off from my wife. "You're a fucking Clarke." Vaeda locked eyes with Colt, and I honestly had no idea what to say. My head was spinning and it was honestly too much to take in. I hadn't even had a cup of coffee yet.

"And you're the man who killed my parents. What the hell are you doin' here? You got some balls showin' up here like this." She stood there slack jawed, and stared at the man who claimed to be my father, before turning to look up at me.

"Greyson, what is this? What's goin' on?"

34

Fuck if I know.

"I just came to meet my son. But things just got a hell of a lot more interesting," Colt said, running a greasy hand through his equally greasy hair.

Just then, another Harley pulled up behind Colt's bike, and revved it up before cutting the engine. The man took off his black helmet, and stared over to where we were standing. He looked to be around my age, and his sleeves were rolled up to his elbows, revealing full sleeves of tattoos on each arm.

"You good, Pa?" the man called out, and lifted his sunglasses to the top of his shaved head. Colt jerked his head to the side to signal for him to come over, and I was getting more and more confused by the moment. *Pa?*

"Greyson, the baby's going to be awake any moment, I can't have this happenin' with her inside," Vaeda whispered into my ear.

"Go inside and lock the door. I'll be okay. I'm just gonna see what the hell they want." Vaeda's sharp blue eyes pleaded with mine, and I could tell she was nervous. "I'll be okay. I promise," I assured her, as she backed into the house and turned the lock. I stepped further out onto the steps, and bent to pick up the cigarette butt Colt had dropped and stuffed it into the pocket of my sweats.

"Drifter, meet your half-brother, Greyson. Greyson, Drifter," Colt said, coolly.

"Sup?" Drifter asked with a head nod, like it was no big deal. *I have a brother? A blood brother?* Drifter looked me up and down, seeming unimpressed with my appearance that was so much unlike his own.

"How old are you?" I asked, realizing how damn young he looked. He didn't look much like me, besides our matching cool blue eyes. We both must have gotten that from our so-called father.

"Seventeen," he said, puffing his chest out. Colt patted Drifter's shoulder as he reached into his pocket to pull out his pack of Marlboro cigarettes.

"Drifter here is my VP of the Grim Reapers," he added after a pause, as if I hadn't already done my research. Colt Davis was the president of Kentucky's largest MC, called the Grim Reapers. Their MC alone was one of the most dangerous in the country, responsible for dozens of deaths every year. Of course, none of them actually served time, as they covered their tracks up pretty well.

"Okay that's great, and as much as I would love a family reunion," I mocked sarcastically, "I really need you to cut to the chase so I can go back inside to my wife and daughter."

"*Daughter*, huh? Would ya look at that, I'm a goddamn grandpa. Fuck," he chuckled, lifting his cigarette back up to his lips.

"You're not and you never will be a grandfather to my daughter," I said through clenched teeth, puffing out my chest and taking a step forward to close the space between us. He smiled crookedly, his eyes dancing with amusement.

"Right," he took a step back. "Well, I just came here to pass the throne. I've got stage-four colon cancer, and I ain't got long. And you bein' the first-born son of mine…tag you're it. It's all yours if you want it," he said, holding his Grim Reapers jacket out from his body, as if it were some sort of medal. I furrowed my brow and looked at him like he had three dicks.

"You've gotta be kidding me. Do I look like a biker to you? I'm a fucking football player." This whole thing was humorous, really. Drifter's thin lips curled into a half smile, as he looked up to his father and cocked his head to the side, as if he was saying 'told ya'.

"Yeah, we thought you might say that. We did our research too," Colt said. Colt turned to face Drifter and punched him playfully on the arm. "Looks like it's all yours when I kick off, Kid."

"So, that's it?" I asked, more than a little confused. Colt shrugged his shoulders, backing off from the steps.

"Yeah. You're my first-born so I had to offer it to you first. But Drifter here's made for this shit. You know…the prodigal son. No offense."

"None taken."

"But Greyson," Colt started again. "Keep your wife close. I already took two Clarkes out in my day. I'd take a third, but I dunno if I got it in me. Drifter here, won't be as forgiving," he warned. Drifter cocked his head to the side, as if he had no clue what he was talking about, until his expression froze on something behind me. I turned to see Vaeda peering out through the glass on the door.

"No shit," Drifter muttered more to himself than to either of us. "You married a Clarke."

"Hey, fuck you!" I shouted, lunging at him, and jabbing my pointer finger right into his chest. "If you even fucking *think* of messing with my family, I will end your life, you hear me?! I may not have grown up a Davis, but I sure as shit have the wrath in my blood, you hear?" Drifter chuckled venomously as Colt stepped in between us as if he were some sort of fucking mediator and not the one who literally just started an entire war.

"Now isn't the time. The time will come. Soon. Let's go, Drifter," Colt said coolly, before turning on his heel and walking to his bike with his puppet following behind him.

"Oh and Greyson?" Colt called over his shoulder. My eyes peered into his, ice on ice, and my fists worked hard at my sides. I wanted to hit him. Break his fucking jaw. *Break something.*

39

"If you know what's good for you. For her. For your daughter…*leave her.* Davis' don't fuck with the Clarkes. And they sure as shit don't mix blood. You'll make yourselves a walking target." And with that, they were off. Just like that.

Chapter Six

Vaeda

Then: Nineteen years old

Of course Lennon would wake up as soon as I gathered enough courage to attempt to eavesdrop through the front door. It didn't work. I couldn't hear nothin' over Lennon's high-pitched squeals. She was up most of the night, and although Greyson attempted to help soothe and rock her, he just got in my way. It wasn't his fault. He always tried to help, and his bond with Lennon was undeniable. I couldn't ask for a better father for my daughter, so I didn't know what my problem was. Everythin' he did got on my every last nerve. I was irritable all the time and I often even found it difficult to bond with Lennon. All I seemed to want to do lately was just lie in bed and sleep my days away. Goin' to school and tendin' to

41

a baby and a house was no easy task. I just didn't have the energy for it all. No amount of coffee seemed to help.

"Do you ever stop cryin' little one? Hmm? Mama's here," I said and she squealed as I lifted her out of her crib. My heart felt heavy and I didn't even know why. I had everythin' I could've ever asked for. A husband who loves me and always makes sure I'm taken care of. I'm fulfillin' my dream to become a surgeon, the one and only thing I've ever wanted to do. I have a beautiful daughter. Lovin' and supportive family. So what the heck was missin'?

As I treaded down the stairs, I heard the front door slam shut. Thankfully as far as I could see, Greyson was still in one piece, but the look on his face was one I'd never seen before. He looked…scared. Broken. Defeated. Lost.

"Everythin' alright?" I asked, swallowin' the giant bowling ball in my throat.

"Yeah. Everything's fine," he muttered, unconvincingly. Lennon started cryin' again, and I swayed with her in my arms, tryin' my hardest to soothe her.

"WAH! WAH! WAAAAHHHH!"

"Oh my God, baby. What the hell is the matter? You just never stop cryin' do you?" I was gettin' frustrated. I swear this baby cried more than she breathed. All. She. Does. Is. Cry.

"Here, let me see her," Greyson offered, holdin' his arms out to take the baby.

"No, I've got it. Just leave us alone." Greyson flinched at my words, and furrowed his brow.

"Are you okay? You've been so moody and *different* since giving birth to Lennon. Maybe you need to see your doctor. Get it figured out."

"Are you kiddin' me right now? I'm not the problem here. Why don't you tell me what the hell that was all about, hmm? Why did Colt Davis just show up on our doorstep? Have you been talkin' to him? Cuz I swear to God Greyson, if you have anythin' to do with those low-lifes, I'll leave and take Lennon and you'll never see us again." The silence after my statement was deafening. My heart was poundin' with fury in my chest, and I could tell my words had shocked him. They shocked *me*. His face hardened, and I thought I saw his eyes fill with tears. It was quick, but it was there.

"I'm going out," he said, turnin' around to leave through the front door.

"Good! Run away like you always do! You're no man. No husband. No fuckin' father!" I shouted after him, tryin' to hurt him as bad as his walking away had hurt me. As he headed toward his truck, he ignored me, and that pissed me off the most. I could feel myself beginning to break. I didn't mean it. I didn't mean to be so cruel. I didn't mean for any of this. I don't know what had come over me. It's like I was another person half of the time, a person even I didn't recognize anymore. Surely, sleep deprivation had gotten the best of me. I just needed to sleep and I would be better. Do better. A loud animal like noise escaped from deep within my chest, and I broke the hell down. Sobbin' uncontrollably, right along with my daughter, as I rocked us both side to side in an attempt to be strong. For her.

Chapter Seven

Greyson

Present day

After the shit-show, and birthday party that I didn't make it in time to, I took Lennon back to my apartment I'd rented in Gator Hill like I did most weekends when I could make it back from Nashville. It wasn't easy splitting my time in two different states, living two completely different lives. I was the star quarterback in Nashville during the week, and a fuck-up father in Alabama on the weekends. I felt guilty about being so far away from my girl. When she got sick in the middle of the night with a high fever and was puking her brains out, I was five hours away, and couldn't make it to the hospital to be with her. I wasn't there for any of her first days of school. I wasn't there when she'd lost her first tooth or learned to ride a bike. I wasn't there for most of it. And part of it was because I was living my lifelong dream, but most of it was to protect them.

For the past five years, ever since I took my dream job with the Tennessee Titans, Vaeda had resented me. She never wanted to hold me back from my dreams, but I also knew she also didn't want to leave the only home and family she'd basically ever known, which was understandable. Not that I gave her much choice in the matter. Taking her with me wasn't an option. It was all part of the plan. I needed to distance myself from her in order to try and dim the static electricity that always ran rampant through my veins when she was around. I'd spent years before that trying to fuck up my marriage. I turned into the piece of shit she always thought I was to begin with, and she was right. I was. *I am.* But one thing I would never in a million years do is walk away from my daughter. I didn't see her nearly as much as I would like, but I made time. I made sure the two of them had everything they could ever want or need, and I stayed the hell out of Vaeda's way. Even if it killed me to do so. Even if I wanted to puke at the sight of the man in the mirror staring back at me.

"Daddy?" Lennon asked, as her blue eyes flickered open. I tucked a strand of her dark hair behind her ear, and smiled at the most beautiful girl I'd ever known. She was Vaeda's twin at that age, and it melted my heart and shattered it all at once. She had her own room here, but at midnight every night like clockwork, she'd stumble into my room to sleep with me in my bed. I knew she was getting a little old to be sleeping with me, but I didn't have the heart to tell her no.

"I'm right here baby," I whispered.

"Do I have to go home today?" Sunday mornings were always so hard. I hated to leave her when I'd barely gotten any time with her. I always took her on either Friday nights or Saturday mornings, and I had to take her back to her mom's on Sunday morning, so that I could make the dreadful drive back to Nashville to start my week. It was a cycle that was trying and hard, but it had to be done.

"Yeah, baby. You do. Daddy will come and get you next weekend and we can do something fun like go to the zoo or something. How does that sound?" She pulled her bottom lip between her teeth, sat up in the bed, and looked away from me.

"I was invited to my friend's birthday party next weekend. Mama said I could go, but that I had to ask you first." My heart fell to my knees, and I hated to admit that I always knew this time would come. When she got a little bit older, and wanted to spend her weekends with her friends. But what the hell could I do? Be the bad guy and say no? As selfish as I wanted to be, I just didn't have the heart.

"Oh. Okay. That's okay. I can come and get you the weekend after that." She nodded her head, and looked up at me with her large, sad eyes. They turned a deeper blue when something was bothering her, just like her mother's did.

"Sorry, Daddy."

"Don't be." I checked my watch, and the corners of my mouth curled into a wide smile. "Do you know what time it is?" I asked in a deep voice.

"No! No, I have to pee!"

"It's TICKLE TIIIIMEEE!" I growled, and scooped her up into my arms and tickled the shit out of her like I'd done since she was a baby. She'd always been so ticklish, just like her mother.

"No! No!" she yelped between laughs. "Dad!" I stopped tickling, and peered deep into her icy blue eyes.

"What did you just call me?" I asked, half joking and half really shocked.

"I mean Daddy," she quickly corrected herself. She'd never called me 'Dad' before. I'd always been Dada or Daddy, but right now, in this moment, it finally dawned on me that she was getting older. Growing up. Gone was the little curly haired girl who trotted around in nothing but a diaper, and here in front of me was a mature eight-year-old girl, who wanted to go to friends' houses and had a mouth full of adult teeth. I knew she wasn't yet a woman, and I cringed at the thought of when that day would come. But she still wasn't my little baby anymore, and it hurt my heart to think of all that I'd missed.

Chapter Eight

Vaeda

Present day

I normally waited inside and watched through the window for Lennon to come inside from her father's newly decked out Audi. I didn't know why, but today I decided to busy myself outside tendin' to the garden. I'd already watered the flowers and trimmed the hedges once this mornin', but I was fidgety and wanted to be outside when she came home. Why? I have no idea.

My belly flip-flopped when I heard the loud sports car comin' up the road, and the deafening bass of the music that was always blaring when he pulled in. I pretended not to notice when he'd pulled in, until I heard the car go silent, and I saw a large, masculine looking shadow hoverin' over me in the grass. I squeezed my thighs together, as I could feel the heat rushin' straight to my groin.

"Can I help you?" I asked, tryin' to keep my voice level. Lennon was busying herself on the sidewalk with her chalk, and didn't even bother comin' to say hello. She was getting older now, and I'd noticed a slight difference in her maturity lately. She no longer wanted bedtime stories or cartoons. Now she wanted to play with friends, polish her nails, and listen to music. I'd overheard her talkin' to one of her friends a few days ago on the phone, and they were talkin' about a boy. *Kissing* a boy. I'd lost my cool and snatched the phone right out of Lennon's hand and hung up on her friend. I'd grounded her from the phone for two weeks, and while some might think that's a little extreme, I only was tryin' to protect her. When I was that age, I was bein' bullied by a certain boy, who made me not want to be in my own skin at times. I didn't want that for my daughter. At eight years old, she shouldn't even be lookin' at any boys.

"Lennon says she's going to a friend's house next weekend?" he asked, his voice soundin' husky and deep.

"Yeah. I mean, if that's okay with you. I figured you'd be happy to save the trip," I said, knowin' damn well I was bein' passive aggressive.

"The drive means nothing to me when it comes to my daughter, Vaeda," he said, narrowing his gaze in on me, makin' me feel incredibly uncomfortable. I could always tell when he was lookin' at me by the way my body would heat up, feeling like an internal fire blazin' through my flesh. I pulled all of my hair over to one shoulder in an attempt to cool myself.

"Well," I cleared my throat, suddenly eager to dart in the house and put some distance between our bodies. "Weekend after that should be fine."

"Right. Well, I was coming up next weekend anyway. My folks thought it would be a good idea if I went with them to see Dotty. Mom says she's fading pretty quickly." He cocked his head to the side tryin' to seem gentle with what he knew was a sensitive topic. The hot blood in my body instantly ran cold, and I had to steady my breathing. Dotty was fading fast. There wasn't a damn thing I could do about it. I'm a doctor, but I can't fix her. I couldn't fix my parents. Or Lennon. What was even the point? I could save other people, other families. Strangers. But no one who really mattered to me. I felt helpless.

I nodded my head and looked away, focusing my gaze on Lennon still drawin' away on the sidewalk. It appeared to be some type of flower.

"I thought maybe, we could get together while Lennon's gone. You know...talk." I looked back to my soon-to-be ex-husband and pinched my brow together.

"What is there to talk about, Greyson?" It felt so normal, yet unfamiliar at the same time, havin' his name roll off of my tongue. I usually just called him 'Lennon's dad' if I referred to him at all. The sound of his name, sent shivers down my legs, and I could feel the goosebumps formin' along my bare thighs.

"A lot. There's a lot I want to say. So much has happened, Vaeda..." A flash of guilt came over his face, and his clear blue eyes darkened just a shade. I wasn't sure if it was the clouds comin' through or if it was his mood. Mine did that sometimes and so did Lennon's. Dependin' on our moods, our eyes would change. They'd light up to the color of clear water when we were excited, or darken to a deep stormy sea when we were upset.

"Alright well…just call first, I guess," I said, crossin' my arms over my chest to appear nonchalant, like his presence didn't set my soul on fire. Would he always have this effect on me? Even when we're divorced? *Fuck, this was annoyin'.*

"Will do. There's a nasty storm coming through, so go ahead and get her inside. We all know how frizzy your hair gets when it rains." *Ugh. What a dick.* It was true though. And with that, he walked to his car and drove off.

Right on cue, a roll of thunder rumbled through the air, and tiny specks of raindrops danced down onto my still burning skin.

"Lennon, come on, honey! It's startin' to rain!" I called from where I was standin' by the garden.

"Hold on, Mama! I'm almost finished!" I sighed and walked over to where she was fiercely drawin' on the sidewalk, and admired her artwork. There wasn't much my baby girl wasn't good at. She was always an excellent artist, despite her lack of excitement toward her art set. She

54

was practically a genius in school, an amazing athlete, and a hell of a singer. I was damn proud to be her mama that was for sure.

"What is it, baby? What kinda flower?" She tilted her head to the side, inspectin' her work thoughtfully, before addin' a touch of a deeper pink shade to the inside of the flower.

"It's an azalea," she said, proudly. I smiled as I pursed my lips together, a ripple of sadness comin' over me. My dear friend, Lennon's favorite flower was always azaleas. It was the type of flowers I brought to her in the hospital when she was sick. I'm not sure if it was in my head, or if it was just the name, but sometimes I really felt like Lennon really was a part of my daughter. Just certain things she would say or how much she cared and had the ability to show compassion. It was a bittersweet thing, and right now, I couldn't help but really crave the advice and wisdom of the only true friend I'd ever really had. If Lennon were here right now, she'd tell me to quit bein' a pain in the ass, and to go make things right with Greyson. She always had the ability to see right through our bullshit and fights, and know that there was somethin' much stronger, much more real behind it all. *I really fuckin' missed my person.*

Chapter Nine

Vaeda

Then: Nineteen years old

"Why did I do this to myself, Dotty?" I wept as she cradled me in her arms, and rocked me right along with her in the recliner. I would never be too big for Dotty to rock, she'd always told me. Even at nineteen years old and a hundred and fifteen pounds.

"Why would I put myself in a position to be hurt like this? I blame you," I said, jokingly through my tears. I didn't really blame Dotty for anythin', but it made her and me both chuckle.

"Me?! I didn't make ya marry that boy."

"Well no, but you made me live right next door to him. What did ya think was goin' to happen?"

"Well, for years I thought you two hated each other. Thought for sure one of these days one of our houses would go up in flames from one of your guys' God-awful pranks. Though I always suspected there was more to it than that, I have to admit." She winked at me as she ran her long fingers through my dark hair, and *shhh'd* me as I cried.

"There, there dear. It's his loss and you know it. If he can't love and accept you at your worst, then he sure as hell doesn't deserve you when you walk across that stage in a few years and knock us all on our asses with your success. You hear me?" I nodded, wantin' to believe what she was tellin' me.

For the last month or so, all Greyson and I seemed to do was fight. He'd go out all hours of the night if I'd even looked at him wrong. He could never fuckin' stay and have a conversation. There was no communication what-so-ever in our so-called marriage. After him yellin' at me countless times to go to my doctor to see what was wrong with me, I finally did, and low and behold, they told me that I was sufferin' from postpartum depression. I wasn't dumb. I did my research, and I knew that was probably the case, though I hated to admit that it had become my reality.

ALEXIS BICE

So I got started on a low dose of medication, for my daughter, and it seemed to be helpin' some. Until now.

But today, when I got back from Lennon's six month check-up, I'd noticed that Greyson had packed everythin' he owned and moved out. I'd called him several times with no answer, so I finally called Aunt Annette to see what was goin' on. I knew she'd answer, and it embarrassed me to no end to let her in on our troubles. And sure enough, she'd told me that Greyson was there and had moved back home. She said we all needed to get together and discuss visitation for Lennon. It pissed me off that Greyson couldn't tell me himself, and that I was hearin' all this from his mama. What a damn child! Surely we'd had fights since Lennon had been born, but ever since his father came to visit over a month ago, things had gone downhill and fast. He still never told me why he came to visit, or if he'd been in contact with him. Anytime I'd brought it up, he'd shut me down and tell me it was none of my business and that he didn't want to talk about it. He'd just given me the cold shoulder, and was never there to comfort me when I was feelin' low and depressed. He still helped with

59

Lennon when he was home, but even their relationship seemed to dwindle. It's like he'd flipped a switch within himself, and turned into a sad, cold man I didn't even recognize. Even when we were younger, he wasn't like this. He'd always been an asshole and a bully, but at least he was givin' me attention when he picked on me, even if it was negative attention. Now he just seemed like he didn't care at all. No emotion. I found it hard to even see why he ever married me in the first place. The man who had let his guard down and loved me so fiercely at one point, though briefly…was gone. And now all that remained was a stranger in the form of my "husband".

Chapter Ten

Greyson

Then: Twenty years old

The day was hotter than balls, and I wiped the dripping sweat from my forehead with the back of my hand. Now that school was out for the summer, I was bored out of my mind without football. My parents carried me through school and took care of everything I needed for Lennon and myself, but I still decided to pick up a summer job serving ice cream at Bobby's Ice Cream Parlor about a mile away from my house. It worked out nicely and kept me busy in the afternoons and weekends. Vaeda and I didn't really have a set schedule with the baby yet; I just took her when I wasn't working, and Vaeda took her when she wasn't working her job at a local diner serving breakfast. Vaeda usually kept her most nights, because she already had the nursery set up at our old apartment, and I didn't really have the space at my parents' house, since God forbid they change around Shamus' old room. Shamus hadn't been home in over two years, and I knew my parents missed him and were worried outta their minds about him. They still kept in contact and talked on the phone almost daily, but I had nothing I wanted to say to him. As far as I was concerned, he wasn't my brother. He was still in Nashville, making his dreams happen, but from the hurt I could see in my mom's eyes, I knew he was still on drugs and booze. I didn't ask and I didn't want to know. I wished he would just fall off the face of the earth, and stop putting our parents through hell.

It was only ten in the morning, and I didn't have to be to work for another few hours, so I decided to pick up Lennon and take her over to Liam's. I hadn't seen or heard from him in a couple of months, and he never answered his damn phone or texted back, so I decided to just show up. I was worried about him, and needed to keep myself busy, rather than just sitting home and letting my thoughts eat me alive. I pounded on the door for what felt like twenty minutes, and Lennon was getting heavy in my arms, so I decided to turn the door handle and let myself in. He never kept the door locked.

"Jesus," I muttered, my nose instantly filling with the most God-awful smell. The place was a shit hole and I know for a fact there was no way his parents would let him live like this. He'd moved out a year ago into his own place, and I had no idea how he could afford this nice of an apartment. It seemed to me like it was a pretty big waste, since it was a shit hole on the inside, and he clearly wasn't taking care of it. There were piles upon piles of clothes strewn throughout the living room, and the only thing besides that and dirty dishes and beer cans, was a giant flat screen T.V. and a futon with a cheaply made coffee table, duct-taped together on one leg.

"Yo, Liam!" I yelled, not feeling like playing hide-and-seek today.

"Ah fuck," I heard someone mumble, and assumed it was him from upstairs. I heard shuffling, and a minute later, he came down the stairs, looking just as disheveled as his house.

"What the fuck man?" I asked, referring to the dump he was living in. His hair was a mop of snarled brown hair, and he was wearing nothing but a silk red robe, with his chest exposed. His eyes were squinted almost shut, and I wondered if he was high right now. As he neared the landing of the stairs, I noticed a little blonde trailing behind him, wearing nothing but a t-shirt and underwear. Clearly I had interrupted something, and I felt extremely out of place, especially with my one-year-old daughter.

"Hey man, what's up?" he asked, letting out a chuckle as he strode across the living room and into the kitchen to grab a beer.

"Seriously? It's like ten o'clock in the morning," I said.

"Ah, but it's five o'clock somewhere, right?" he shot back. "Oh, Greyson, this is Megan," he waved a loose hand in her general direction.

"Meegan," she corrected, folding her tan arms across her chest, looking embarrassed.

"Right. Whatever. Anyway, what brings you here?"

"Well, I hadn't heard from you in a coon's age, so I thought I'd bring little Len over to see Landon. But apparently, he's not here."

"Nah, he's with CeCe. I had a busy night," he added winking at Meegan. Liam took a long swig of his beer before slamming it onto the granite countertop and started shuffling around the kitchen opening and closing cupboards. I found it odd that he hadn't acknowledged my daughter, or even looked at her once.

"Fuck, I need to get groceries," he slurred, walking back into the living room and plopping down on the futon, bringing Meegan with him.

"Dude…are you okay?" I asked, hoping he wouldn't take offense to the question especially in front of his guest.

"Hey, go take a shower and I'll be in a minute, 'kay?" he said to Meegan, who got up from the futon, before taking a slap to the bottom.

"Hey, man. Everything's good. Never been better actually," he said, looking me square in the eyes. His eyes were bloodshot so I knew he'd been drunk, high, or crying.

"The fuck man, are you stoned?" I accused, seriously wondering who the man was sitting before me, and wondering where the hell my best friend went. He'd been distant ever since Lennon died, and I knew he was partying a lot, but I didn't know things were this bad. His place was a dump, his cupboards were empty, and I knew from others that he was sleeping his way through town.

"Stoned? What are you a tween? Weed is for pussies," he replied, cocking his head to the side as his lips curved into a crooked grin.

"So you're a druggie now?" I said with disbelief. I couldn't even believe what I was hearing. Liam was always so against drugs. Mainly because Lennon was against them, and never even dabbled into pot in high school. But I knew he never did either, aside from pot once with me, and when Lennon found out, she'd flipped. He seldom drank since Landon was born. He didn't need to. He'd had everything he'd ever wanted. There was nothing he needed to numb. Until now…

"Druggie?" he chuckled. "I wouldn't say that. I'd call it more like living on the edge every once in a while.

The fuck do I got to lose anyway, Greyson?" he added, his face becoming more somber.

"Um, I don't know. Your son, maybe?" I retorted with disbelief. He couldn't be serious.

"My *son* is fine. And he's also none of your business. I never hear from you anymore, so why don't you take your high horse and shove it up your ass. Your judgment isn't welcomed here." His jaw was clenched tightly, and I could practically see the smoke coming out of his ears. He was pissed, but I didn't fucking care. He needed to be told when he was in the wrong, and if his parents or no one else was gonna do it, then I would.

"Please tell me you're not serious," I snapped, just getting started. "Your *son* is also my *Godson*, in case you've forgotten. So he kind of is my business. And maybe you'd hear from me if you'd ever answer your damn phone or reply to any of my countless text messages. And my *high horse?* Just because I'm not a fucking druggie doesn't mean I think I'm all high and mighty, Liam. Jesus, grow the fuck up." Lennon started to fuss in my arms, and I'd almost forgotten I was holding her while I was spewing venom at the friend who had clearly turned into a stranger. I could tell nothing I said mattered to him, and he just let my words bounce right off him like I meant fucking nothing. So I turned to leave, since I clearly wasn't welcome.

"Oh and Greyson?" he called from behind me. "Next time you knock Vaeda up…don't name it after my dead fiancé." I shot a glance behind my shoulder at him, completely floored by what he'd just said. His green eyes had turned ice cold, and I knew now wasn't the time.

I had no idea he'd had an issue with us naming the baby after Lennon. She was Vaeda's best friend and my best friend's fiancé. He'd never voiced his concern before now, and although he never really asked how she was doing, he seemed to love her when she was born. He'd held her a lot in the beginning, and always brought Landon over to hang out. The babies would chill in their bouncers while watching some cartoons, and Liam and I would talk or throw ball. But a couple months ago, he'd stopped coming around. Stopped answering my calls and messages. He just kind of fell off the face of the earth.

When I got back to the house, I was undoubtedly bummed. It was hotter than a whore in church outside, and there was nothing to do. My old man was working on the ranch and my mom was working at the hospital, as usual.

I plopped down on the sofa with Lennon and stared into her big, beautiful, blue eyes. My heart clenched in my chest, and I could feel my breathing hitch. *This* is what I didn't want to do. I loved my daughter with all of my heart, but it's what I saw in her that cut me to my fucking core. It hurt me in ways I never thought possible. It always put a damper on my mood and sent my mind running a mile a minute.

"Da!" she yelled, placing her plump little hand on my cheek, making everything better. That's all it took to make all my worries fade and to remind me why I'm doing this.

"Yeah. I'm your da, baby girl," I said, swallowing the tightness in my throat.

Chapter Eleven

Vaeda

Then: Nineteen years old

The mornin' was already pipin' hot and it was only early June. My thighs were stickin' together in my diner uniform of a white polo and matchin' mini skirt. The uniform was hideous, but at least it made me look tan. I was naturally tan, but the white really contrasted to my golden-bronzed skin. Greyson normally took Lennon while I worked my mornin' shift, and I grabbed her from him while he worked his afternoon shift. But Greyson wasn't answerin' his phone, so I left her with Dotty, and she'd texted that Greyson *just* picked her up at 10:00 a.m. When I would be done with work in an hour. *Ugh*.

Winston's Diner was finally clearin' out from the mornin' rush, and I was relieved to finally be able to take my time sweeping and mopping before closing. The AC

70

had shit the bed yesterday morning, and I'd had a hell of a morning catchin' the heat of everyone's complaints. *Yes, I'm sorry the AC isn't working right now. No, I'm sorry I can't just go and get a new one. The owner should be here shortly to have a look at it.* Not to mention I'd served three six tops this morning that didn't even leave a dime for a tip.

I wiped the beads of sweat off from my forehead with the sleeve of my polo, just when I heard the buzzer go off. I turned, relieved that it was probably Winston finally comin' to fix the AC, just when my heart sank and my flesh heated up further. *Emma Blake, Harper Lennox, and Caleb Streeter.* Great. Just my damn luck.

"Oh, looky who it is. Thought she was going to go further after high school than just waiting tables, but guess that's what happens when you have a baby after graduation," Harper sneered, causin' Emma to throw her head back with laughter. Caleb just smirked at me, before takin' a seat at the only table that I had yet to clear off from the last customers.

"Excuse me, waiter? Can you please get this garbage off the table and get me a sweet tea?" Caleb called over to me.

"Make that two," Emma added.

"Three actually. Lemon wedge in mine and only half-filled with ice. Crushed." I couldn't help but roll my eyes in complete and utter disbelief at this bitch's audacity.

"We only have cubed ice. Sorry," I shot back, clearin' the table off with as much as I could grab in one trip.

"Then crush it," she ordered, with a fake smile planted on her freshly glossed lips. *How about I crush your plastic lookin' fuckin' face, Barbie?*

After their table was cleared and freshly wiped down, I came back with my notepad, only to see that they'd moved tables. *Seriously?* I stood in front of their table, waitin' to take their order while two out of the three stooges clicked away on their cell phones. I cleared my throat, causin' Harper to snap her head up at me with a scowl.

"Nice outfit, Miss Diner Girl. Y'know, you look much better with your clothes *off*," she winked, makin' fun of me as she looked me up and down. I could feel my cheeks burnin' with heat at the realization that she must have been talkin' about the sex tape that had circulated through the whole school. How could I forget?

"We should have edited it to put a couple extra pounds on her, she's looking a little thin these days. Times must be hard," Emma mocked, taking in my full appearance.

"Ladies, play nice," Caleb scolded, plantin' a kiss on each of their lips. *What in the hell? What were they a throuple now?*

"What are you talkin' about?" I shot at them.

"What? You seriously didn't know that it was us who took that video?" Harper chuckled, seemin' pleased with herself. "Your *baby daddy* left his phone in the hallway. We saw him chase after you like his little puppy had just gotten loose, and we couldn't help but want to watch and enjoy the show."

"Yeah," Emma chimed in, cozyin' up to Harper. "We could have all joined in. Spiced things up a bit. It looked pretty *vanilla* to me."

"Right? I can't believe Greyson's into that. He was *far* from vanilla with me," Harper added, twisting the knife further into my gut. The final blow to my heart.

"You guys are unbelievable," I bit, shaking my head at them, when what I really wanted to do was flip the table over. I spent all that time bein' angry at Greyson and accusin' him of bein' the one to record and send out that video, when I knew deep in my heart that it just wasn't him. But nothin' else made sense. And now, after all this time, I find out that it was *them?* It made sense now. Kind of. Emma and Harper have always had some sort of grudge against me because of their weird obsession with Greyson, but…Caleb? What did he have against me?

"Why, Caleb?" I asked, soundin' more pathetic than I'd meant to. But I needed to know. He looked up at me, his hooded gaze meeting mine.

"Oh baby, don't be upset. It was all in good fun, wasn't it girls?" Emma and Harper nodded in unison, their smiles makin' me want to claw into their pretty little faces.

"Out!" I shouted, causin' them all to jump. "Now! Get out!"

"Ugh, you can't do that. We're paying customers," Emma scoffed.

"I SAID GET THE FUCK OUT!!!"

Just then, the buzzer went off, and we all turned to see Winston, the owner, standin' in the doorway. His mostly bald head was glistening with sweat, and his beer belly was hanging below his white cutoff. I knew by the look on his face that I'd better start lookin' for another damn job.

Chapter Twelve

Greyson

Then: Twenty years old

I'd barely just gotten back to the house when the front door slammed shut and Vaeda stormed in, looking like she was ready to kill someone. I swallowed hard, fully aware of how damn attractive she looked when she was pissed off, and especially in that tight little white uniform she wore for work that made her skin look like a bronzed goddess.

"I can't believe this! I'm goin' to kill those three psychos!" She paced back and forth across the length of my living room, and the scent of freshly brewed coffee and cinnamon rolls warmed my nose each time she walked past me.

"Whoa, whoa. What's going on?" I asked.

"I just lost my job," she said, planting her feet in front of me, before filling me in on the story of how Emma Blake, Harper Lennox, and Caleb Streeter showed up to her job and basically sabotaged her. I didn't believe for one second that they didn't know she worked there. It was all too perfect. But why now? Why after all this time would they come back and reopen that can of worms? I don't know, but I sure as hell was going to find out.

***

I kept Lennon for a while longer while Vaeda went to apply for a new job. I played it cool until she picked up our daughter, and then it was go-time. Last I knew, the three musketeers had skipped town and moved to another state, I think Kentucky for whatever reason, but now they were back. I did a little research, and found out where they were living. All three together were renting an apartment, not more than three blocks from Vaeda. *How convenient, eh?*

I ran up the front steps to their townhouse apartment, and banged my fist on the door as hard as I could, and I didn't let up until it opened. *Just the face I wanted to see.*

"Greyson Tucker, what's up man?"

"You motherfucker!" I charged at him full force, not holding anything back. Okay, maybe a little, because I had a daughter to think about, but not much. My fist made blow after blow to his pretty boy face, causing his signature slicked back hair to fall into his eyes. I punched and kicked, taking all of my years of pent-up anger out on him. I pounded him bloody, until I felt at least some of the anger leaving my body. I gathered myself onto my feet, panting and out of breath, and not bothering to help him up. He looked every bit of the pathetic piece of shit that he was, as he lied there, squirming like a bug that had just been stomped on but not yet killed. I looked to my left and saw the two blondes standing there in awe, just watching everything unfold.

"You girls need help. All three of you do," I said, looking from them to Caleb, who was now attempting to sit up, still clutching his stomach. He spit blood on the floor, and I smiled wickedly at him.

Just then, "Give Me Back My Hometown" by Eric Church started playing on Harper's phone, and she stepped away to answer it.

"Hey, Bossman," she answered, before her voice faded off into the distance. Emma's eyes met Caleb's and I couldn't tell what it was I saw in their eyes, but it made me feel uneasy. She took two steps forward and reached a long, thin hand out to help him stand up.

"I want answers…and where the hell is my old phone?" I barked at the two of them.

"Phone's gone man, just let it go."

"Let it *go*? What are you *high?*"

"It was a long time ago!" Caleb said, smoothing his hair back with his hand.

"You're right. It was. But you guys are the ones who came back and ever-so-conveniently showed up at the diner where Vaeda works, just to rip the Band-Aid off and spit in the wound. *You* did this. Not me," I pointed a finger at his chest, feeling the anger within me beginning to resurface. Not that it ever really left, but thoughts of my daughter kept creeping up on me and reminding me of why I could not break every bone in this douchebag's body and go to jail.

"Look, we didn't know she worked there, man. We just wanted a hot meal after a long night." He winked at Emma, who rolled her eyes, seeming unfazed.

"Right. So explain to me why you even took the video in the first place? And then just decided to send it to every single fucking contact in my damn phone? Do you know how humiliated she was?!" I spewed, having to restrain myself from decking him again. *Think about Lennon. Just think about Lennon.*

"I'm sorry, man. I honestly thought she already knew it was us. I swear we meant no harm," he said, holding his arms up into a surrendering gesture.

Just then, Harper came back into the entryway where the three of us were standing, and she looked like she'd just seen a ghost.

"Boss is in town," she said in a small but serious tone. Caleb remained silent for a moment, his expression remaining calm.

"Okay then. We've gotta run. We're done here, right?" he asked, locking eyes with me. I squinted my eyes at him, clenching my fists, once, twice.

"Don't let either one of us run into any of you again," I said, looking at all three of them. "And I fuckin' mean in." And with that, I turned the brass door handle, just in time to come face to face with…*my goddamn father.*

Chapter Thirteen

Greyson

Then: Twenty years old

"Hello, Greyson. Long time no see." He cocked his head to the side, and his lips curled into a half smile.

"What the fuck are you doing here?" I asked, looking behind me at an equally dumbfounded Caleb and two bimbos.

"I've come to check on a couple of my employees. See if they're uh…holding up their end of the deal." Colt's eyes locked with Caleb's, who looked like he was four and half seconds away from shitting his pants.

"We're working on it. I told you that." Colt snickered under his breath, before running his hand through his scraggly goatee.

"Use that tone with me again," he paused, shooting daggers with his eyes. "I will lay your ass out on your own front lawn. Ya hear?" Caleb's eyes widened with fear as he nodded his head frantically.

"Yes, sir."

"Good." Colt turned his attention back to me. "If you'll excuse me, *Son,* I have some business to attend to."

"What business?" I asked, really fucking confused. Was that the 'Bossman' who had just called Harper's phone a few minutes ago?

"Nothing. Because I'm out," Emma said, as everyone's head turned to her. She stood there in her pale pink mini skirt and matching camisole, covering her thin, pale arms over her chest.

"Aw, that was cute. Nice try," Colt said.

"I'm serious, Colt. I'm done. I'm going back to my parents'. I'm nobody's *bitch,*" she shot back, sidestepping in front of Colt to try and get through the doorway. Colt made no move to let her through, and she stood staring up at him, her eyes barely coming up to his nipples. Colt held her chin in between his thumb and pointer finger, and smiled widely, before he kissed her right on the lips.

83

"You're not done until I say you're done. Now turn that perfect little ass around and go get your Bossman somethin' cold to drink. It's been a long ride." I shook my head, just as Colt pushed his way into the doorway, knocking me out onto the front steps.

"And Greyson? Don't forget our last talk, Son," Colt said, before shutting the door behind me. My heart sped up with fury, anxiety, and I don't even fucking know what. What the hell was all that? *Don't forget our last talk?* How the fuck could I? I did what he'd said. I destroyed my fucking family. I left my wife. To keep her safe. But what the hell was he doing back in Gator Hill? And what kind of business were Caleb, Emma, and Harper doing with him? I guess that would explain why they moved to Kentucky. But then…why come back? What was 'their end of the deal' that Colt mentioned?

I stewed upon my strange as hell afternoon all night long, until I finally decided I needed answers. I didn't want them. But I needed them. And I knew there was only one person who I even had the slightest chance of getting information from. And that was Emma Blake.

Chapter Fourteen

Vaeda

Then: Nineteen years old

Nobody would hire me because I didn't have enough experience. I applied and talked to several restaurant managers knowing full well that the restaurant bizz was the only way I'd be able to make enough money while attending school. I needed tips. How the hell was I supposed to gain experience if nobody would hire me? It took every ounce of integrity I had, but I had no choice but to call Winston back and apologize, and beg for my job back. He actually sounded relieved to hear from me, bein' that I knew we were already short-staffed to begin with. There were only two waitresses, me and Connie, a fifty-somethin' year old who always reeked of booze. I'm pretty sure she and Winston had a side thing goin' on, but I tried not to pay much attention. It wasn't my business, and I was just there to do my job and get paid. Winston agreed to give me my job back, but I was back on 'probation'. I had to treat each and every customer with the utmost respect, regardless if they tipped or treated me like garbage. I couldn't friggin' wait until I graduated school and became a doctor. All these low-lifes would never be able to treat me like dirt again. I would provide a good life for my daughter, and me, and nobody could threaten to take that away from me again. Not even Greyson. I wouldn't need his help. I wouldn't need help from anybody.

As I was layin' in bed that night, I couldn't shake this odd feelin' that somethin' was wrong. I couldn't put my finger on it, and it was the strangest thing. Lennon was fast asleep – for now, but here I was wide awake, tossin' and turnin'. I sat up and turned my bedside lamp on to double check that I'd taken my antidepressant meds, and I did. So what the heck was wrong? I turned the lamp back off and plopped my head back on the pillow and tried to get comfy. This was gonna be a long night. My chest felt heavy and my heart was racin', and I didn't even know why.

After scrollin' through Pinterest for what felt like decades, and pinning recipes I knew I'd never try, I finally started to doze off.

I woke up to a loud bang, and sat straight up in the bed and checked my phone, only to realize it was 2:00 a.m. My mouth was dry and felt like I'd swallowed a cactus in my sleep, so I chugged the remaining water on my nightstand before standin' up to check on the baby. I wasn't sure what the bang was, but I think I remember hearin' it was supposed to storm tonight. I tiptoed down the stairs to peek out the window when I noticed that the front door was open just a crack. I'm sure I closed it when I got back from pickin' up Lennon from her dad's. Did I forget to lock it? I peered out the window, and sure enough, it was pourin' sheets of rain. The trees swayed in the night breeze, and it looked darker than usual out. The blackest of black took over the night sky, and it looked eerily peaceful. Except, I couldn't swallow the lump that was stuck in the back of my throat. Why was the door open? I shut the door and turned the lock, and darted back up the stairs to check on Lennon. I tiptoed over to her crib, willin' the floor not to creek, so as not to wake her. But all I saw was…*an empty crib.* Nothin'. She wasn't there. I flicked the light switch on, my heart punchin' through my chest, and I felt like I was gonna faint right then and there.

"Lennon!" She was only a year old, and I knew for a fact, she hadn't mastered climbin' out of the crib yet.

"Oh my God." I ran rampant through the entire apartment, lookin' for somethin' I knew I wasn't going to find. *She was gone.*

I dialed Greyson's number, and as soon as he answered, I could tell that he was asleep. He didn't have her. I bent over and clutched my knees, the phone droppin' to the floor, as I threw up into the trash can in the corner of the room.

"Vaeda! What's going on?!" I heard him shout through the phone speaker. When I finally felt like there was nothin' else to throw up, I picked the phone back up, and wiped my mouth with the back of my hand.

"Lennon's missin'. Please. Please tell me you have her, Greyson." But I knew. I knew he didn't.

"WHAT?!" he roared, "that motherfucker!" I heard ruffling on the other end of the phone, and I assumed he was gettin' out of bed to come over just when the phone went blank and he'd hung up. I paced around the length of my apartment, searchin' for anythin' that I could find. Any clues, anythin' that could tell me what might have happened. I didn't find anything. The only thing was the door that was open just a crack. Nothin' was out of the ordinary. Nothing at all.

After twenty minutes or so, Greyson still wasn't here. I dialed, and dialed, and dialed him again, but with no answer.

"What the fuck, Greyson!" I shouted, chuckin' my phone at the wall. Where the hell was he? What could possibly be takin' him so long, when his daughter was missing?!

Unable to wait around for him any longer, I did one more sweep of the entire apartment, checkin' every crevice and corner, makin' sure she really wasn't here, before I jumped in my car and took matters into my own hands. I started driving towards Greyson's house, havin' to drive

89

with my high beams on because it was so dark out. My hands were shakin' and slidin' all over the steering wheel from the sweat on my palms. Just as I rounded the corner about three blocks from my apartment, and one block from Greyson's, I squinted my eyes, seein' what looked like his truck parked at one of the newer townhouse apartments. It was next to one of the ones that Shamus had lived in before he fled to Nashville. I slowed my speed, comin' to a crawl in front of the line of apartments, when I saw the football sticker in the back window, and I knew for a fact it was Greyson's truck. What the hell was he doin' here? Who even lived here? I didn't even shut my car off, before I jumped out and ran full speed up to the door. I pounded my balled up fist as hard as I could against the wet door, until finally, it opened. And there stood Greyson, barefoot, his eyes watery and wild, holdin' our baby girl.

Chapter Fifteen

Greyson

Then: Twenty years old

I called Emma a handful of times and texted a dozen times, but to no avail. She wouldn't answer. So I took matters into my own hands, and drove over to her parents' house. When I pulled up, I made sure to leave my high beams on, shining right through what I knew was her bedroom window, until I saw the curtain shift to the side, and her head peer through the window before darting outside.

"What the hell are you doing here?! You're going to wake my parents up!" She yelled in a hushed tone. I motioned for her to get in the truck, before I drove off, headed to I don't know where. I just drove and drove, my hands clutching so tight to the steering wheel that I thought it might snap off.

"Talk," I said, in a sharp tone.

"I have nothing to say," she said in a small voice, her hands fidgeting in her lap. She was nervous. She knew what I wanted to talk about. I knew I wasn't letting her out of this truck until I got some damn answers.

"What does Colt Davis want from you? Why are you working with him?" She looked down to her lap and twisted around a diamond bracelet she was wearing. It was a nice bracelet, and it looked like it cost a lot of money. A lot of money that I knew neither she nor her parents had. She shrugged her shoulders.

"It's just business. A job. It's how I make ends meet."

"Doing *what* exactly?" I urged.

"It's just business," she repeated. "Why don't you ask him yourself? He is your father." I slapped my open hand on the center of the steering wheel, embracing the sting I felt that quickly turned into a burning itch.

"He's not my fucking father! He's a crooked man, Emma. What does he want from you? Why did you move back here, and what the hell is he doing in Gator Hill?!"

92

Emma peered out the window, searching for the words to say. She better search a little fucking faster, because I was running thin on patience.

"He doesn't want you with Vaeda. Something about his and her family. A long history of rivalry, which I'm sure you already know." Her voice was low, and I could barely hear her. She turned her head back to look at me, and looked scared. Of what? Of Colt?

"Well, as you know, Vaeda and I are not together. So what's the issue? What's his plan?"

"I can't tell you that." My fingers grasped the shifter, and I almost pulled it off. I could physically feel the rage shooting up to my chest from deep within my knotted stomach. I would never ever hit a woman, but I'd be lying if I said I didn't want to throttle her right now.

"Damn it, Emma! This is my fucking life he's messing with! I have a daughter!"

"Then protect her!" she yelled, as if it were obvious. "Run. Take her and run, Greyson. Colt will be dead in a matter of months. He's sick. But until then, if you want my advice, you should go." Her eyes glossed over with a fresh coat of tears, and I certainly wasn't expecting that to come out of her mouth. What was this, a fucking horror movie? I wasn't going anywhere. I already transferred schools from Ohio State to University of Alabama. My life was here. My daughter was here. I couldn't just rip her away from her mother. As if Vaeda would ever go for that. If there was one thing I was sure of it was that Colt Davis didn't scare me. I might have left Vaeda to protect her and our daughter, but enough was enough. He would not fuck up my life any more than he already had.

After I dropped Emma back off at her parents' house, I drove and drove and drove some more, to nowhere in particular. I needed to release the fire from my body, and I knew if I went home that my mother would start questioning me. She always knew when I was angry or upset. I was in no mood to talk. So I let my truck take me down all the back roads I'd forgotten even existed, while blaring any music that wasn't my brother's as loud as my speakers would allow.

When I finally cooled down some, I found my way back home, and tossed and turned in bed for a good forty-five minutes, before actually falling asleep. I had an eerie feeling that I couldn't quite explain, and I couldn't shake it. I couldn't explain it even if I'd wanted to. I just couldn't help but feel that Colt was warning me from something…*bigger*. My chest just felt heavy and my mind was racing a mile a minute. I scrolled through Facebook, looking at Vaeda's profile, and once I clicked on a picture from 2009 and accidentally liked it, I decided it was time to make myself fall asleep.

I woke up in the middle of the night to my phone vibrating against the lamp on my bedside table, and when I checked to see who the hell was calling me at 2:00 a.m., I realized it was Vaeda. My heart fucking sank.

"Hello? I answered, groggily, though my heart was skipping every other beat making me feel like I was going to pass out in my own damn bed. I heard what sounded like vomiting in the background, and I instantly panicked.

"Vaeda! What's going on?!" A moment later, I heard her muffled cries come through the speaker.

"Lennon's missin'. Please. Please tell me you have her, Greyson."

"WHAT?! That motherfucker!" I couldn't think. I couldn't speak. I hung up the phone without even realizing I did. My lips felt numb and I was shaking so bad I wasn't sure how I even slipped a pair of pants on and ran to my truck. It took me until I reached my destination and jumped out of the truck to realize I wasn't wearing any shoes. I ran up to the door and turned the brass knob. To my surprise, it wasn't locked, and I busted through it like I owned the damn place.

"Where is she?!?!" I growled. "Where's my fucking daughter?!" It was pitch black in the apartment, even more so because it was storming like a motherfucker outside. A lamp turned on from within the living room and I heard my father's voice come through, loud and clear.

"Hello, Greyson. I've been expecting you." My eyes darted to where he was sitting and fury burned through every part of my flesh when I saw that he was holding my baby girl.

"Oh, you're gonna die, you sonofabitch!" I lunged forward and plucked Lennon out of his grimy hands before taking my opposite arm and using it to swing full force against his skull. It wasn't as much damage as I wanted to do, but I was holding my daughter, and that was more important right now.

"Nice hit!" he snickered, appearing to be reveling in the pain I knew he must have felt, since the side of his head was bleeding from the blow. I hadn't even noticed Caleb and Harper sitting huddled together on the couch, looking like they were snuggled up for date night, and not a part of a goddamn Amber Alert.

"You better start talking now before I call the police and beat each of you nonstop until they get here."

"Oh, stop the dramatics, pretty boy. I just wanted to see my grandbaby," he said, his voice sounding all paternal, which was the furthest thing from reality.

Just then, I heard a pounding at the door, and I whipped it open to see Vaeda was standing there, soaked to the bone. *Shit, I wasn't even thinking about her.*

"Greyson, what the hell!" She charged into my chest, and peeled the baby out of my arms.

"Aw, look who it is. Mama Clarke."

"Shut your mouth, Colt," I warned.

"Y' know, Greyson. When you learned of your true identity, and our family history…Did you really think it would be a good idea to mix oil and water? I mean come on…you can't be that stupid, son."

"What? Is that what this is about? You came into my house and *kidnapped* my fucking daughter because you think your blood is mixed with mine?" Vaeda spewed, her face contorted as if the idea of our blood mixed together was repulsive. It confirmed my biggest fear that she saw me as nothing but the product of my father. *A Davis.*

"Vaeda…Don't." My eyes pleaded with her. I didn't want to hear it. I saw it every goddamn day. It tore me up inside. Ate at my fucking flesh.

"What, Greyson?! It's true and you know it!" She turned her attention from me to Colt. *Don't fucking do this, Vaeda. It's not true! She's mine!*

"She's not his biological daughter!"

Chapter Sixteen

Vaeda

Then: Eighteen years old

I couldn't believe it. Two pink lines stared back at me as clear as day. Positive. I was pregnant. I had made a baby while I was black out drunk with the love of my life's *brother*. How could I be so stupid? How could I have been so careless? One stupid decision. One careless encounter. My life was changed forever. Where do I go from here? I'm supposed to be a surgeon. Medical school is no joke. Eight friggin' years of my life is supposed to be dedicated to my education and my future! How will I possibly be able to juggle a new baby into the mix? I wasn't sure, but I knew it had to be done. There was no way I would get an abortion. I would never.

After hours of tears and going back and forth in my bedroom, clutchin' the framed picture of me and Rufus, right before he took his last breath, I knew what needed to be done.

I pounded my shakin' fist against the door that I hoped I would never walk through again. A minute or so later, Shamus answered the door, wearin' nothin' but a pair of blue jeans with his red and white boxers peekin' through the top. His shoulder length hair was a mess of dirty blonde, and his eyes were bloodshot. I felt my bottom lip tremble as he opened the door wider and allowed me to come inside. The apartment was just as messy as it was two months ago, if not more so. There were pots and pans clutterin' the marble countertops, fallen ashes on the coffee table, and the place reeked of booze and body odor. Shamus had always showered and appeared clean, so this was new territory to me. And it made me sick to my core, with what I was about to tell him. What my life was about to become. *With him.* I would give anythin' for this baby to be Greyson's. Or even anyone else's. This truly was my worst nightmare.

"What's wrong with you, Kid?" he asked, lookin' me over from head to toe.

"Shamus…we need to talk." He walked over to the refrigerator, and grabbed two Budweiser bottles off from the top shelf, and handed me one. I shook my head.

"No, thanks." He cocked his head to the side and furrowed his blonde brow.

"You mean you didn't come here to kick back and have a couple brews?"

"No. I didn't. I came here to tell you that…that I'm uh. I'm pregnant. And it's yours. It's definitely yours," I murmured, tossin' over in my head all the different ways I possibly could have said that. His tanned cheeks turned instantly ashen, and his bloodshot eyes were opened wide. He looked like he'd just seen a ghost, and I wondered if he was even breathin'.

"Shamus…say somethin'." The silence was killin' me. I could hear my heartbeat through my ears, and it sounded like drums. No matter how long I stared at him, waitin' for him to say something…anything…no words came out. He just sat there, starin' off into the distance.

"Are you gonna talk to me?" I urged, getting slightly freaked out.

"Look Kid, I can't raise a baby. I mean, look at this shit hole. You wanna bring a baby up in this?" I looked around at the dirty clothes, and the filth that he was living in. He had a good point, but my baby still deserved a father, even if it was...*him.*

"Well, I'm not sayin' we should be together. We could share the baby. Fifty-fifty custody or visitation even...I mean, what other choice do we have?" He pulled his lips into a tight line, and looked me square in the eyes.

"You could always...you know...get rid of it." *What?* He couldn't be serious. He did not just say that to me. No way, no how.

"You're kidding. Please tell me you're kidding, Shamus." But he wasn't. I knew he wasn't.

"Vaeda. I'm sorry that things between us crossed the line. I've always liked and respected you, and your aunt and uncle have never been anythin' but good to me. But I cannot be a father. I've got a life to build for myself. I live for my music and nothin' else. I'm selfish and I know I am, and I'm not ready to change that. I'm sorry, Vaeda, but if you have that baby, you're on your own." And those were the words that would haunt me for eternity. This was my life. One bad decision had cost me everything. Now I had no choice but to suffer the consequences. I was about to be a single momma, raisin' a baby on my own.

"Shamus, come on. This isn't exactly what I had in my mind for my future either, but we did this together. How am I supposed to raise a baby on my own? This baby needs a father!" Hurt displayed openly on his face, but it couldn't have compared to what I was feeling. Hurt was an understatement. Everything would change for me. *Everything.* And Shamus just got to run off and play his stupid music and not even think twice about the tiny human *he* helped create.

"I'm really sorry. You won't be alone, and you know that. You have Dotty and Henry, and…my brother. If there's anything I know about my brother, it's that he's always loved the shit outta you. He'll step up to the plate. Be a better man than me. Don't let me hold you back from anythin', Kid. I just can't be a part of it. I've been talkin' to my manager and I'm leaving for Nashville in two weeks. I've got a name to make for myself, y'know?"

And he did. But his name was a name I vowed to myself to never speak again.

Chapter Seventeen

Greyson

Then: Twenty years old

I always knew it. I mean we hadn't had sex at all around the time she'd gotten pregnant. I was in college in another state, living the dream. Then Liam called me and told me that Lennon had died, and I rushed back here to Gator Hill, and found myself caught up in a mess that I never would have dreamed I'd be in. But when Vaeda told me she was pregnant, I already knew that Shamus had fled to Nashville for his music. I knew my brother and I knew he wouldn't let anything stop him or get in the way of that. He was selfish. Always had been, always would be.

It was an unspoken truth, something that we'd never spoken of out loud before. Vaeda tried to change my mind. To stop me from packing up and moving my life back to Gator Hill and taking on a responsibility that wasn't mine to have. But it was. Vaeda was mine. She'd always been mine. And that baby, blood or not, was fucking *mine* too. Always would be. I was Lennon's father, regardless of whether Vaeda and I were together or not. From the moment she told me she was pregnant I was there. Every ultrasound, every baby appointment, every move she made, I was there. Watching her be born was an experience I could have only dreamed of. I cut her umbilical cord, I signed her birth certificate, and I even chose her middle name. Elizabeth. Both Dotty's and my mother's middle names. I doubt our families had ever figured out that Lennon wasn't my biological daughter. She looked so much like Vaeda in her hair, colorings, and eyes that there really wasn't much of Shamus. But every once in a while, she would make a facial expression or a gesture, and I saw it clear as day. My brother. My enemy. *A stranger.*

It cut me to the core in ways I can't explain, hearing those words come out of Vaeda's mouth. I understand why she did it, but it didn't make it any less painful. If Lennon was a target because Colt assumed she was Davis blood mixed with Clarke, then I would do whatever needed to be done to keep her safe.

Colt cocked his head to the side and smiled.

"No shit. Clarke women have always been little whores," he said, as he ran his hand through his beard. "Your mama used to run around in nine inch heels and cut off booty shorts, just askin' for cock." Vaeda passed Lennon back to me and hauled off and smacked him hard across the face, so quick even I didn't see it coming. It was an impressive hit, really.

"Don't you ever talk down about my mama. You don't know nothin' about her! She was my daddy's entire world and he was hers."

"Yeah. You might be right about that, but she's dead now. And if I remember correctly, her last words were…*Please don't do this. I have a daughter*," he mocked, savagely. Vaeda's jaw dropped open, and I heard a sob catch in her throat. That motherfucker. How could someone be that evil? How was that even humanly possible? Was I capable of that kind of malevolence? Could I say and do the things that my father had done too?

LOVE YOU MOST

My biggest fear since learning my true identity was that I could have it in me to be like him. To be evil. To hurt people. Especially Vaeda. I already had the rage in me since I was born. It would come out at different times, and it was hard to control it. It burned through me like a smoldering flame, burning out of control, and destroying everything in its wake. I'd never be able to live with myself if I ever hurt her. And that's why I knew that leaving her was the right decision. As much as it killed me inside not to wake up next to her every morning, I knew keeping my distance was the right thing to do. Every doubt I'd ever had, every time my knees weakened and I wanted to buckle and cave in, and run straight into the arms of the only woman who had ever made me feel *something*, it was all gone now. I did the right thing. For me. For her. For us. And especially for Lennon. Whether I liked it or not, and despite who'd raised me, I'd always be my father's son.

Chapter Eighteen

Vaeda

Then: Six years old

"There's my pretty little princess, lookin' even more cute than she was this mornin'," Daddy said, as he walked into the kitchen after doin' 'business' with his club. My daddy was the biggest, baddest thing around, and he was pretty dang important. To me, my mama, and everyone else. He often told me bein' prez of the Dead Riders was no easy task. That's why he was so busy all the time. But that's okay, because I had my mama. She stayed home with me every day and always took good care of me.

"Here you go, peaches and cream with a heaping scoop of vanilla ice cream," Mama said, as she placed my bowl of dessert in front of me. It was Mama's favorite treat and mine. Mama always liked to eat pretty healthy, but like me, she had a sweet tooth too.

"Mmm, it's so yummy," I said after fillin' my mouth full of the warm, juicy fruit.

"Hey, Princess, I got a surprise for ya. When you're done eatin'." My eyes widened and a smile spread across my cheeks.

"What is it?! Tell me now, tell me now!" I chanted, excitedly. My mama looked at him with her 'what did you do now' look that she always gave him.

"Alright, come on outside," he said. I stood up from where I was sittin' at the kitchen table, and followed my parents outside, hardly able to contain my excitement. When I walked outside into the prickly, dry grass, I screamed as loud as I possibly could and jumped up and down a hundred-zillion times.

"A dog! You got me a dog! Mama, look it! Daddy got me a dog!" I couldn't believe it. It was a dream come true. I'd begged for as long as I could remember for a dog, and Mama always said it was too big of a responsibility. But really, I just don't think she liked dogs all that much.

"Oh, Amos," Mama said to Daddy, before I ran up and plucked my new puppy out of Uncle Will's hands.

Uncle Will was my Daddy's best friend and VP of his motorcycle club and they did everything together.

The puppy was so small and fluffy and his fur was the color of golden sand.

"Woof! Woof!" the dog yelped in between his soft licks on my cheek.

"Well, Princess, what are ya gonna name him?" Daddy asked, ignorin' my mama's concern written all over her face.

"How abouuuuuut…Rufus!" I exclaimed. "I always liked that name for a dog."

For the next two weeks, my new best friend Rufus and I did everythin' together. We were stuck like glue just like Daddy and Uncle Will. I had to go back to school and start first grade, but he was right there waitin' by the door for me when I got home. He waited patiently while I did my homework, and we played and played and played some more until bedtime. He even sat outside the bathtub while I took a bath, and sometimes I even shared some of my dinner with him. Mama said I wasn't supposed to feed him table food, but he seemed to like my vegetables a lot better than I did. He needed vitamins too so he could get big and strong and live forever and ever.

It was Saturday morning and my parents were arguin' about somethin'. I wasn't sure what. They didn't really argue a lot unless it had to do with my daddy's club. I know my mama didn't like him on the road all the time, but that's how he made his money so we could have lots of nice things, he always said. Most of the time they were all cuddly and gross and super in love. Daddy says I'm never allowed to kiss boys the way he kisses my mama, and that was fine with me, because that was disgustin'.

An hour later, Mama came into my room and said that Tatiana, the girl who babysat me sometimes, was gonna come and watch me and play for a little while, while she and Daddy went on a business trip. She said they would be back really late and not to wait up for her. I didn't want her to go. I didn't like bein' left with Tatiana. Tatiana never played with me. She was always so nice to me until Mama left, and then she would just ignore me and play on her phone or smoke grass and eat all of our food. I don't know why she liked to smoke grass, but I guess that's what you do when you're an adult. I saw my daddy smoke grass once with Uncle Will, and it made him laugh a lot. *Whatever. Grown ups.*

As usual, when Tatiana showed up, she pretended like she was the nicest girl in the world. She nodded to all of Mama's instructions, and even kept runnin' her hand through my pigtails like we were best friends or somethin'.

"Okay, baby, remember what I told you. Mama and Daddy are going to be back really late, so don't wait up, okay? You be a good girl."

"But Mama, I don't want you to go. Do you have to? Why can't you just stay home with me?" I started to cry, and I really hated cryin'. It made me feel weak, and Clarkes were far from weak, Daddy always told me. I never saw my parents cry. Never ever.

"Princess, we'll be back in a little while. You gotta be brave, Vaeda. I know you don't like it when your mama leaves, but you're brave. When you wake up in the mornin', I'll make us all some blueberry pancakes and bacon, okay? Your favorite. We'll spend the day out by the pool and even teach Rufus some new tricks," Daddy said as he ran his thick hand through my hair, and it made me feel a little bit better. I nodded, even though I still didn't want them to go. I didn't know why, but I just felt so sad about it and it made my stomach hurt.

As usual, I played alone in my room with Rufus, and Tatiana ignored me and smoked her grass and ate all my favorite cookies and fruit snacks. She didn't even give me dinner or make sure I took a bath, so I snuck some vanilla ice cream into my room and a can of peaches that I didn't know how to open, so I just ate the ice cream.

But when the next mornin' came, and I ran into my parents' bedroom, I saw nothin' but an empty bed that was still freshly made. I ran downstairs, and saw Tatiana was still here, and she was on the phone. She was pacin' back and forth across the living room, and she sounded upset.

"Where's my parents?" I asked, tryin' to hold back my tears from spillin' down my cheeks. She hung up the phone and looked at me in a way that I never wanted to be looked at again. *Sorry. Pity.*

"Oh, Vaeda, I'm so sorry. I'm so, so sorry."

"Why? Where are they?! When are they comin' home?!" I shouted. I never was mean to Tatiana, but I just wanted my dang parents. They said they would be here! We were supposed to have blueberry pancakes and bacon for breakfast and spend the day by the pool! We were supposed to teach Rufus how to do tricks! Where were they?!

Tatiana shook her head, her long purplish-pink hair swayin' from side to side.

Just then, I heard a motorcycle pull up in front of our house, and I felt so dang relieved. There they were. Just in time for breakfast. I was starvin'. But when I whipped open the front door and ran out onto the front steps, I saw that it was my Uncle Will. He took his helmet off and started walkin' toward me. I didn't move. I didn't say anything. I don't even think I was breathing.

"Hey there, pretty girl," he said, his bottom lip wavering. His eyes were all red and puffy and he looked like he'd been cryin'. His black hair was all messy from his helmet, and he looked really tired. He was dressed in the same black leather jacket that my daddy always wore, except I noticed he was holdin' another one in his hands.

"What's that, Uncle Will?" I asked, tryin' to be brave. *You gotta be brave, Vaeda. Be brave.*

"It's your daddy's jacket, sweetheart. I'm givin' it to you, because. Uh…fuck," he shook his head and tears started rollin' down his bearded cheeks. "I'm so dang sorry, little girl. So dang sorry. Your parents were in a really bad accident." He looked up and his eyes met mine, and I saw how sad he was.

"They're gone, sweetheart." And that's the moment that my life changed forever. Just hours ago, I was sittin' in my room eating ice-cream out of the carton without a care in the world, and today I was an orphan.

"What? Gone? Where? Where are they? Where did they go?! We have to go out to the pool! I wanted to swim! I wanted to show Rufus tricks! I want…I want…I just want my parents!!!!!"

Chapter Nineteen

Vaeda

Then: Nineteen years old

Despite the pleas from Harper and Caleb not to go to the police, and the handsome amount of cash they'd offered me to keep quiet, I did what I knew I had to do and went to the police. I'd reported everything that happened, and the two officers I'd spoken to just looked at me like I had four heads. There was nothing they could do since I hadn't reported Lennon missing before I got her back, and she was unharmed. I couldn't believe they weren't willing to help me. To arrest them. To do *something* at least. So I filed a restraining order against all three of them. Though I knew if they ever came near my daughter or me again, I would kill them with my bare hands. I was my daddy's daughter after all. I was a fuckin' Clarke. *And Clarkes are not weak.*

LOVE YOU MOST

The night had been exhausting to say the least. I didn't even feel safe in my own home anymore. School was already out for the summer, and I needed change. I could always move back in with Dotty and Uncle Henry, but I didn't want to burden them. Calista was already givin' them a run for their money at twelve years old.

After much thought, I knew what I needed to do. I told Greyson my plan, out of respect for him bein' Lennon's dad, and although he didn't agree with me, he understood. It would just be for the summer until I had to go back to school.

After hours long of drivin' and two different stops for iced coffee to keep me awake, I finally drove into the bright, beautiful town of Sunnyside, Alabama. Where I was born. My home until I was six years old. Despite bein' so young when I left, I still remembered almost everythin' about this place. It was called Sunnyside for a reason. Every building in this town was painted bright and fun colors. The entire main street was done in different shades of yellows, just like the sun. I didn't know why, but I hardly ever remember it raining here. I'm sure it must have because it would only make sense, but I have no memory of it raining at all when I was a child. The sun was always out every day, beatin' down and warmin' my skin while I played in the dirt.

Just bein' back here, already made me feel more at peace. Maybe it was the bright sunshine, or maybe I felt closer to my parents, or even the busy atmosphere of people bustling by on their bikes or jogging, with long lines of sweaty children at the ice cream shop with their grass stained knees. All of it made me so happy. I felt at peace. I felt *at home.*

A sudden pang of sadness came over me as I looked across the field of the local park. Kids were tossin' Frisbees to their excited dogs, and I suddenly found myself really missin' Rufus. I'd always missed my dog, but bein' back here, where my journey with him started, was a whole new grieving process, or so it felt like. I'd been lucky enough to share twelve long years with him by my side, bein' the most loyal and trusting friend I could have ever asked for. He'd died of old age, and he wasn't in pain. For that I was grateful. He'd been a lot less active in his last months of

119

life, so I knew that the inevitable was eventually comin'. I woke up one mornin', Rufus at the foot of my bed like always, but he didn't wake up when I stirred. And I just knew. I'm just glad he spent his last moments by my side, and I hoped he was learnin' those new tricks my daddy was gonna teach him. I hoped they were together waitin' for me.

I took a deep breath, filling my lungs with the fresh air that smelled like fresh grass and grilled food. The entire street was packed full of little eateries of some of the best food I'd ever had in my life. I realized now that I'd forgotten to eat before I left this mornin', and I was suddenly starving. Lennon was enjoying the view and people watchin' from her stroller, and I decided to walk down the main street and grab us somethin' to eat. As we walked along the sidewalk, it felt as if we'd lived here all our lives. I didn't feel out of place. I felt as if we actually belonged here. Even if our life belonged to Gator Hill now, Sunnyside would always hold a special place in my heart. My home away from home.

I waited in line at the outdoor window of Sunny's for my burger and fries and a frozen yogurt to munch on with Lennon, when I saw someone kneel down and start talkin' to Lennon right in front of her stroller. My defenses immediately went up after the incident back home, and I was ready to pounce.

"Um, excuse me. What do you think you're doing?" The long-legged brunette, looked up at me, shocked, and immediately started apologizing.

"Oh, I'm so sorry. She was smiling at me, and I just had to come and say hello. I didn't touch her. I'm sorry if that was out of line. She's just too precious," the woman said, lookin' back down to Lennon, who was reaching her little hand out to touch her.

"Oh. Sorry, I didn't mean…"

"No, that's okay. Don't worry about it. Mama Bear. I get it," she said, offering an apologetic smile. "I'm Juliet. It's nice to meet you. Are you new in town? I haven't seen you around before." Juliet stood up from her crouched position, and held a long, thin hand out for me to shake.

"No. Yes. Kind of. It's a long story," I blushed, realizing how stupid I must have sounded. "I'm Vaeda. And this is Lennon."

"Vaeda...I've only known of one Vaeda all my life," Juliet said, cockin' her head to the side, takin' in my appearance.

"I was born here. I moved away when I was little."

"Huh. You didn't by chance go to school at Sunnyside Elementary, did you?" she asked, still lookin' me over. I nodded, a half smile tugging at the corners of my mouth.

"I did. I moved away at the start of first grade. My parents passed away and I went to live with my aunt and uncle in a town called Gator Hill."

"No fucking way," she said, and immediately apologized for cussin' in front of Lennon.

"Vaeda...Clarke?" I chuckled, realizin' how small of a town Sunnyside really was.

"Yep, that's me. I'm sorry, I don't really remember..."

"Oh no, that's okay. I'm Juliet Rivers. I was in your class before you moved. We played together some, but you pretty much kept to yourself." I studied the woman before me, and though she did look vaguely familiar, I didn't remember too many of the kids from my old school. My memories tended to revolve mostly around my parents. Or maybe I just wanted it that way.

"I'm really sorry about what happened to your parents. We all were. Mrs. Laribee and our class wanted to mail you a card, but we didn't have your new mailing address."

"Oh." I offered a nervous laugh, as I didn't really know what to say. Luckily my food was up, and I grabbed my tray and walked over to a nearby vacant picnic table under an umbrella, but I noticed Juliet followin' behind me. Though I wasn't too keen on small talk, I didn't really feel uncomfortable around her either. Lennon had been my only true friend all my life, so I didn't really know what to talk about. I'd never been one for 'girl talk' or gossip. I wasn't sure what Juliet was into and I knew nothin' about her. I kind of just wanted to eat my meal, and go visit the one and only person I came here to see. But I couldn't be rude.

I set my tray on the red picnic table, and placed Lennon by my side, as Juliet took a seat in the shade across from me.

"So, are you going to school?" she asked.

"University of South Alabama. I'm studying medicine. I want to be a surgeon."

"No way! That's where I'm going!" she exclaimed excitedly, like she just found her new bestie, and we'd meet up for coffee and a study sesh.

"Oh yeah? What's your major?" I asked, interested.

"Addiction studies. I'm going to be a drug and alcohol counselor. The whole path of addiction and recovery has always been just so intriguing to me," she said, lookin' thoughtful.

"Nice. Second year?"

"Indeed. I haven't seen you around school. Maybe I will sometime."

We chatted for a while, and I ate my food and fed Lennon some frozen yogurt. I was surprised to find that although I didn't really have any friends, Juliet was actually really easy to talk to. She seemed a bit more upbeat and bubbly than what I was used to, but she was nice nonetheless. We exchanged numbers before I left, and I decided that it couldn't hurt to have someone on my side to talk to every now and again, who wasn't my aunt and uncle or a one-year-old baby.

I got back in my car and drove around for a while, second-guessing myself and my reason for comin' here. But the longer I drove around, the more I knew I needed to do it. I needed closure.

I pulled up in front of the familiar white and black building, and though it had had some updates over the years, it looked relatively the same. The windows were tinted black and the fancy lettering painted on the windows matched the font of the Dead Riders on the back of their jackets. I climbed out and settled Lennon into her stroller, before walkin' over to the group of guys huddled together on their bikes outside the front entrance of the building.

A bunch of them turned their heads and whispered to one another, no doubt wondering who the hell I was.

"Hi. I…um. I'm just lookin' for…"

"My God…Vaeda is that you?" I heard a voice call out, and I looked through the sea of bikers to match the face to the voice.

A tall man with shaggy dark hair made a path through the others and walked toward me. He looked the same as before, except his black hair was now streaked with grey. His beard was longer than I remembered, and he had the same build, tall and stocky, maybe a hair thinner than before.

"Hey, guys. Piss off, I need a minute!" he shouted, and to my surprise, the dozens of guys scurried off into the building without a fuss.

"Look at you," he said, placing his thick, fatherly hands on my shoulders to look me over. His eyes were brimmed with tears, and I had to look away so that I didn't cry too.

"I haven't been back here in awhile. I just wanted to see the place and get…closure, I guess. I think I need that." He nodded, and his expression grew more serious, almost as if he'd expected me to come one day. He was a good

126

foot or more taller than me, and I felt like a child in his embrace.

"Of course. Whatever you need. And this…is this yours?" he asked, referring to Lennon, who was just starin' wide-eyed at the strange man before her.

"Yeah, she is. This is Lennon." I smiled proudly at my daughter; as he greeted her and bent down to ruffle her curls, before leading me into his office. I took a deep breath as I entered the club, not knowin' what I was goin' to feel when I did so. I thought I'd want to cry or feel upset or uneasy, but to my surprise, I felt a sense of complete calmness come over my entire body as I walked through the old, familiar clubhouse. The countertops in the main room were new. The old tile was ripped up and replaced with beautiful hardwood flooring. The paint appeared to be fresh. But everythin' else was the same from the setup, to the atmosphere, to the pool table, and the pictures on the wall of our fallen members. A smile spread across my cheeks as I noticed my father's picture in the center of the wall, with the others surroundin' it. It was just how I'd remembered him. Tall, dark hair, and handsome. Wearin' his black leather jacket, sittin' proud on his Harley. I stared into the eyes that were so much like my own, and I suddenly felt a breeze move past me causin' my arms to fill with goosebumps. I knew my father was with me in that moment, and I knew he would be glad that I'd come back. This was his home. This was my home.

"You're so grown up, Princess. I can't believe it. You look so much like your mother, but I see him in ya too." I smiled at his kind words, and took a seat across from him at the long rectangular cherry table. He sat at the head, where I assumed he always sat for meetings.

"Thirteen years have passed. And yet, in some ways, it only feels like thirteen days. Minutes even. I still remember you showin' up on my doorstep all those years ago. I thought you were my daddy pullin' in on his bike. I was so relieved. Excited." My eyes darted to the floor, and I suddenly felt extremely vulnerable in that moment. I hadn't brought up that fateful day in years. Although I always remembered my parents, I always tried to only think of the good life we'd lived. I never liked to think about what actually happened or why. Not even when Greyson told me the truth about his birth parents and Colt admitting to their murder. I was angry, sure. Livid. But I still didn't really let myself truly *feel* it all. For two weeks when Dotty came to stay with me at my parents' house, before takin' me back to the ranch, all I did was cry. But then in a sense, I was ripped away from my home and everythin' that I'd ever known, and was made to start fresh. Dotty was only doin' all that she could. And of course, if none of that had happened, I probably would never have had Lennon, or met my best friend Lennon. They say everythin' happens for a reason, but I knew it was time. Time to finally get the full picture on why my parents actually died. I couldn't shut it out any longer. I am a part of them, and they will always be a part of me.

"I remember it all too well, Kiddo. I still beat myself up, thinkin' of other ways or things I could have said when I delivered that news. I wanted to be the one to do it, but sometimes I think it wasn't my place." Our eyes met, and I shook my head.

"No. I'm glad it was you. You were the closest family I had aside from my aunt and uncle, but they were hours away. In a sense, you were my second father." He smiled at my statement, and I fisted my hands at my sides, suddenly feelin' a tad nervous.

"But I want to know what happened. And why. I know the rivalry between the Clarke and Davis families. But I'm sure there's just so much more that I don't know. And I'm ready." Will pursed his lips together and nodded, before sittin' up straighter in his leather chair.

"You sure?" he asked, his expression solemn and stern. I nodded in response.

"I'm sure."

"Okay. Fair enough. So you know that your great-grandfather, Lyle Clarke, killed Colt's grandfather, Simon Davis?" I nodded.

"But why, though?" He shrugged his shoulders.

"All I really know is that Lyle walked in on Simon screwin' his wife. The two men had never really gotten along. With clubs, it's always kind of a pissing match. Y'know, see who's dicks are bigger." I nodded my understanding. *Guys were always like that. Especially Greyson.*

130

"Your great-grandfather, Lyle, got the Dead Riders involved with the drug-trade business. The Dead Riders worked with the Grim Reapers, who had been in the business for years. I don't know the whole back story, but I figure Simon thought that Lyle was stepping on his toes, and then the whole mess with him getting involved with Lyle's wife. And one thing led to another and he killed Simon. Stabbed him and left him for dead. Lyle got away with the murder, and tension has been high between the two families and clubs ever since.

Your old man...he uh...he was tryin' to get us out of the drug trade. Your mama, she didn't want any part of it, and he knew it wasn't right havin' a little girl and all. So the day they died...we all rode down to Gavenport to the spot where the Dead Riders always met up with the Reapers." Will paused and took a deep breath and swallowed. My palms were sweating, and I rubbed them along the length of my bare thighs to dry them off. Plus, I sure as hell couldn't sit still right now.

"We were in too deep. We owed the Reapers a hell of a lot of money, and if we were out of the drug business, in their eyes, how the hell would they get paid back that kinda money? We're talking hundreds of thousands," he paused to look me in the eye to emphasize the severity of the situation. "So when Amos broke the news to Colt, things went south. Some punches were thrown and some knuckles got bloody, but that was that. We were out. We left Gavenport with a weight lifted off of our shoulders. But Colt didn't head back to Kentucky with the rest of his crew. He followed us, and rode side by side by your parents. There was a tractor-trailer comin' and Colt purposely cut him off, causin' him to swerve into the other lane. They were both killed instantly from the impact." Will's eyes darted to the floor and I realized then that both of us were crying.

"And then what? Nobody sought justice for him or her? Colt just got to roam free and move on with his life while a six year old was left an orphan?" Will's bottom lip trembled and I could practically feel his guilt. It was written all over his face and flooded out of his pores. The air was thick with emotion, and it was almost hard to breath.

"I know. Trust me, Princess, I know. It's haunted me every damn day for the past thirteen years. But all I can do now is try and make your old man proud. I got us out of the drug trade for good. We're a good club that makes an honest living. And word on the street has it that Colt Davis ain't got much longer to live anyhow."

"Yeah, well, much longer is still too long." I wasn't going to, but I felt like I needed to. Will had finally confided in me and told me everything. So I told him everything about Greyson and I and his true identity. I told him about how Colt showed up one day to meet him and then came back to Gator Hill and took Lennon for revenge. I told him about Lennon's biological father...how Colt came back and took Lennon. I told him everythin'.

He stiffened in his chair and didn't say a word for the longest time. The air turned cold and the energy shift in the room was intense. The guilt on Will's face turned into somethin' else. He was completely expressionless, but his previously watery eyes were now dark and hooded. Thankfully, Lennon started to fuss to break the silence.

"So, I was actually thinkin'…I was hopin' that maybe I could find a place to rent out just for the summer, and that maybe I could get a summer job here at the club. You know, paperwork or cleaning or somethin' like that. I don't need much, just enough to get us by. I just…I can't go back to Gator Hill. Not right now. I think Lennon and I just need a fresh start, ya know? Even if it's just for the summer. A breather."

I felt a little awkward just showin' up here outta the blue and askin' for a job, but I knew this was the best thing for us right now. I'd have to find a sitter for Lennon while I worked, if he'd even have me, but that wasn't a big deal. I knew all of my money would just go to payin' rent and daycare for Lennon, but I also knew Greyson would never let either of us go without. I wasn't high maintenance by any means. I painted my own nails. I never got my hair done other than the usual trim, and I never bought expensive clothes.

To my surprise, Will agreed to hire me for the summer to clean and do paperwork and do some 'personal assistant' duties like runnin' errands, etc. As luck would have it, he said it would be absolutely no trouble for me to bring Lennon along. There was no illegal business goin' on in the club anymore, and he said that most of the time at least one or two of the guys' ole ladies came to hangout while their husbands worked, so I would have help with Lennon. He found me a small cottage to stay in that a family friend of his owned, and it was only a few hundred a month, fully furnished. I couldn't help but feel so entirely grateful for how all of this had worked out and practically unfolded into my lap. Things never worked out this easily for me. Ever. Although I'd only be makin' minimum wage, I was incredibly excited to do somethin' different, and to be back in my father's club. His home. His sanctuary. I knew without a doubt that he was here with me, allowin' all of this to happen. I smiled as I stepped out of the club and looked up to the sky. Almost as if on cue, a cloud shifted to the side, allowing the sun to beat down onto my skin, and it was so bright, I couldn't see a thing. In that moment, I don't think I'd ever felt quite as peaceful as I did right then. As I brought my head back down, Lennon reached her arm up toward the sky, as if she was grabbin' onto somethin', and I knew she felt it too.

Chapter Twenty

Greyson

Then: Twenty years old

It was the same shit different day. Wake up and putt around the house, longing for a life that was no longer mine. Alone. Workout. Go to work. Come home. FaceTime with Lennon. Repeat. My days had no purpose anymore. I couldn't just go and pick up my daughter and spend the day with her until I had to go to work. I hadn't physically seen her in over a month. The days were long, and I wasn't sure how much longer I could live like this. It wouldn't be quite as grueling if I at least had football to keep me occupied, but it was summer and there wasn't shit to do.

I'd heard from Liam a couple weeks ago. He texted and apologized for how he'd acted. I didn't even respond. I didn't know what to say. It was as if we had nothing in common anymore, and that made me feel even more alone.

LOVE YOU MOST

I had hundreds of friends in school; except they weren't really *friends*. They were acquaintances. People who loved how I looked or how good I played football. But none of them actually knew me. They didn't know the first thing about me. The only two people who have even gotten a glimpse into the real me were the two people who weren't even in my life anymore.

As I laid my head back and pressed my palms into my eyelids, my phone buzzed in my pocket. Vaeda. I sat straight up, and my heart pounded in my chest, as I internally cussed myself out for being so excited to see her name flash across my iPhone screen.

"Greyson?" she breathed into the phone.

"Y-yeah?" She never called me. She'd texted daily just to let me know Lennon and her were okay, and she would let me FaceTime with Lennon, but she never talked.

"I just called to tell you…I thought you should know…your father…he's…he's dead, Greyson." I remained silent on the other end for a long time, as I processed what she'd just said. Normally when people heard those very words, their lives would crumble beneath

138

their feet. Their worlds would fall apart. A father is a man who is supposed to protect their family. Fathers were the glue that held everything and everyone together. They were supposed to provide for and be there for their kids. Listen and love them. Sons were supposed to look up to their fathers and be proud to walk in their footsteps. To hope and pray to become even half the man their father was. But my father was far from admirable. He was nothing I'd ever looked up to or wanted to be like. My world didn't fall apart or crumble at my feet. If anything, I felt more at peace and more empowered than ever. From the moment I overheard my parents talking about my biological parents when I was just eleven or twelve years old, I hated him. I hated her. I'd never met them, but I knew I never wanted to. When he showed up that one day on my doorstep and threatened my wife and daughter, I had secretly counted down the days until Colt Davis took his last fucking breath.

"Oh. How do you know?" I asked. I took a deep breath, and for the first time, it felt effortless. Like I could breathe again.

"Drifter…your brother…he came by with a couple from their crew and delivered the news and offered a truce. It's a long story, but I know for a fact my dad's club is out of the drug business for good. Drifter's the new president of the Reapers, and he had a talk with Will." Fuck. I forgot about Drifter, my so-called *brother*. Just because my father was dead, Drifter was clearly still alive and more involved with the club than ever. He and my father were two peas in a pod. Had my father left his unfinished business behind for Drifter to take care of?

"Did he…did he see you? Drifter?"

"Yeah. We talked." My heart fell into the pit of my stomach and I felt like my airway was trapped. Blocked off. I couldn't breathe. Think. Speak.

"He was fine. He apologized to me. He said when Colt was alive he had to do as he was told to please him. He didn't say why, or what would happen if he didn't, but you can use your imagination. I actually believe him. I saw him in a much different light than the angry boy who showed up to our apartment with your father." I sighed, and shook my head. I wasn't as quick to forgive him as Vaeda was, but at least he didn't threaten her. I hoped he was telling the truth and that he was a better man than Colt ever was.

"Well, just keep an eye out. I still don't want him anywhere near you or Lennon. Be smart, Vaeda."

"I will."

"Did he...did he say how he died?"

"No, he didn't say. I just assumed it was the sickness. We all knew it wouldn't be long." Yeah, she was right. Now both of my biological parents were dead. Although I never met my biological mother, I knew she was just as bad as Colt. I'd done my research on her too, and I knew that she'd died four or five years ago in a car crash. It was crazy how detached I was from my own blood. I wasn't upset when I read that just like I wasn't upset now. Colt and Renee Davis were not my parents. I was the son of Reed and Annette Tucker. Good. Kind. Sometimes loving. A damn good father. I didn't have to live a lie anymore. I could be with Vaeda. I could have my family back. Suddenly, I felt like I was on top of the world.

My limbs felt weightless and a smile spread across my cheeks.

"So, uh. Does this mean…does this mean you can come home? To…me?" Butterflies danced in my stomach, and I felt like an adolescent girl waiting to hear back from her crush.

"No, Greyson. It doesn't. I'm finally finding myself again, here. Who I am without Greyson Tucker. And I…I kinda like her." The smile on my cheeks faded instantly, and I couldn't believe what she'd just said.

We could finally be together! We didn't have to worry about anyone hurting her or Lennon! We could raise our daughter together again. I mean I know we had some issues before Colt even came into the picture, but we could get past all that. She was on meds now, so she wouldn't be a total bitch all the time. We could be a family. But then again, what if it was still in my blood to hurt her? What if I broke her heart or worse hurt her physically. I don't think I could ever have it in me to hurt a woman, but what if my anger got the best of me one day, if things got heated enough? My mind was a racing battle of what I knew my heart wanted…my family…and what my mind was telling me…to let it go. Find someone else. Co-parent for Lennon and close that chapter of my life. The chapter of Greyson Asshole Tucker and Vaeda Mutt Clarke. But that chapter was the greatest part of my entire story. My whole existence.

"So you don't want your family together? I'm confused…" I wanted her to want me. To want us. *I want us.* But then again, I don't know if I deserve her or deserve us. I couldn't blame her for leaving Gator Hill to find herself. I was hot one minute and then I was ice cold. I know that. But that was my terms. My decision to make. It was always my decision.

"Greyson, you packed your shit and left one day out of the blue. If you're tellin' me it was because you were scared of what Colt might do then that's not the kind of love I want. I want a love that you fight for. A love that you would do anything and everything to protect. A love no matter what, you don't just abandon. I thought I loved you. I thought I needed you. But even before Colt came along, you showed me your true colors. When I was dealing with postpartum depression, where the hell were you?" I could hear the anger rising in her voice, and I couldn't even argue. She was right.

"You would bolt at the first sign of trouble. You always have. You've always looked for a way out. And now…I finally realize I don't need you. We can co-parent for Lennon's sake, but I think we should get a divorce. We aren't happy." *What? A divorce?!*

"You want a divorce? I'm confused. I know I've been an ass. But that's all in the past. I refuse to divorce the one and only woman I've ever loved. It won't happen. Not until we're absolutely sure at least. Just…let's take some time and think on it. Please. Really reevaluate ourselves and our relationship." She remained silent on the other end for a minute, and I knew she was lost in thought. At least she was thinking about it. That's all I could ask for really.

When I hung up the phone, I plopped myself down onto my bed and I just stared blankly at the ceiling for who the hell knows how long. I was lost in thought. One thing I'd never really had to deal with before was rejection. It felt…*shitty.* I was no stranger to pain that's for sure.

Finding out I was adopted, my mother leaving, Vaeda hooking up with my brother, and then getting pregnant. Making the decision to separate from my wife so that she didn't get hurt. That was pain in its truest form. A fucking knife to the throat. It hurt. It still fucking hurts. But rejection? Yeah, that's a whole new territory for me. And I don't like it. I don't like it one bit.

Chapter Twenty-One

Vaeda

Then: Twenty-one years old

I felt peaceful and at ease as I unpacked our belongings into our brand new apartment. It was a fresh start after a fresh start. This summer was exactly the rejuvenation I needed. It reminded me just how much I loved and missed Sunnyside, Alabama, and I vowed to myself and to Lennon to make trips down there more often. But Gator Hill was and has been my home for a long time now. I made peace and found closure with my past, and that's exactly what I needed. Will promised to still keep in touch, and I was sad to leave him and all the other club members and their wives I'd grown so close to, but I had to get back to Gator Hill and start my third year of college. One step closer.

About a week or so ago, I was tidying up things in the shop, ready to lock up and go home, just when no one other than Greyson Tucker himself walked through the front door. I hadn't seen him all summer and the sight of him alone, standin' there in his crisp, white t-shirt, and lookin' all tan made me weak in the knees. He'd driven all that way just to talk and plead with me to move back in with him and give him another chance. I was hesitant at first, of course, but I saw a sense of seriousness in his eyes that I hadn't seen there before. Like he really wanted to try and make it work. I knew he loved me. I knew he was tryin'. But I was deathly afraid of going back in full force and givin' him my everything just to come home one day and him and all his shit be gone. Again. That hurt. Really fuckin' bad. I was Vaeda fuckin' Clarke. I never let anyone or anything hurt me, ever. But Greyson Asshole Tucker, proved that to be wrong time after time. The only one who could get under my skin and make my knees buckle and my stomach ache all at the same damn time. He was the angel on my shoulder and the devil on my back. So much good, but so much wrong at the same time.

"Whatcha thinkin' about, you pretty little mutt?" He stood in the doorway of our new bedroom, holdin' one arm above his head, restin' on the doorframe. I couldn't help but giggle.

"You know, you're the only one who can make somethin' so mean sound so cute at the same time." He shrugged his perfectly square shoulders before waltzing over to me and performing the perfect pirouette before ploppin' himself back onto our freshly made bed.

"Did the football player go soft on me while I was gone?" I teased. "Greyson Tucker, former star quarterback turns into a prima ballerina," I joked, knowin' full well, he was the furthest thing from soft as you can get.

"Vaeda?" he asked, lookin' thoughtful as he propped himself up onto one elbow.

"What is it, Princess?" I played. His eyes dimmed and a low scowl escaped his lips.

"Shut the hell up and sit on my dick." My eyes widened in response, and my thighs clenched together, feelin' the heat rush through my body. It was such a change of pace, but it was so...*Greyson*.

148

"I have to finish unpacking before Lennon wakes up from her nap." I was instantly aware of the nervous flutters swarming in my belly and my breathing quickened. I hadn't slept with Greyson or anyone for that matter in months. It was a long, hot summer without any release. I was suddenly aware of how much I craved it. Craved him. He sat up and inched closer to me, and took the stack of folded t-shirts out of my hands before tossin' them on the floor. I stood frozen, unsure of what to do next. I was caught off guard. I didn't know if I should fight him off and continue to unpack, or surrender to the desire buildin' up in every inch of my flesh.

"Vaeda…it's been a long summer of fucking my fist to your memory. I need to feel you. To taste you. I'm fucking starving for your body." He slipped his thumbs inside my shorts and slid them down my thighs. Goosebumps from his touch formed along my legs where his hands had brushed. Longing for more, but knowing it was too soon. We still had a lot of talking to do, and I needed to unpack, dammit.

"Ugh, Greyson," I moaned, knowing full well how this was going to end. He stood up before me, his tight body pressed against mine. The heat from his body was soothing the goosebumps on mine and making them disappear. With one swift motion, he picked me up like I weighed nothin' and threw me down on the bed. I gasped, and knew then that I was done for. He slid a long finger into the side of my pale pink panties, and ran his finger along the length of my wet folds, before playing at my entrance. I shifted my hips into him, urging him to press further. To fill me. Oh how long it's been…but he didn't. He just made slow, soft swirls right at my hole, never inching further. I was soaking wet and panting with excitement. I was beyond aroused, and needed him inside me. Now.

"Greyson, please," I panted, throwing my head back. He slipped his hand out from my underwear, and I shot my head back up to see what the hell he was doin'. He couldn't just leave me like this! That would be cruel. My sex pulsed at where his fingers had just been, and it craved more. Oh, so much more.

"Tell me you still love me, Vaeda," he growled into my ear. What? Why? Why do we have to talk about this right now? Can't we just... "Say it," he bit, firmly.

"I...Greyson...we can talk after. You know how I feel. Why do you think I'm here?" I mean, duh, what was he, stupid? We already agreed to try and make things work.

"I want to hear you say it." He flicked his hot tongue on my earlobe, and brought it between his teeth. He nibbled softly, alternating between licking and biting, and I couldn't help but wish he was doin' that somewhere else.

"I still..." I paused, tryin' to think clear headedly, but it was damn near impossible right now with the building and impending release of my orgasm on the verge of already shattering.

"Say it," he urged. He trailed soft kisses along my breasts, pushin' my bra to the sides, so that my perky breasts were in his face. He popped a nipple into his mouth and sucked, and I thought I might lose it, right then and there.

"Oh, God. Yes."

"*Now*, Vaeda." He moved his wet lips down along my belly and stopped at the top of my panties. The anticipation of what he was going to do next was slowly killing me. *Please, more. Now.* He slid my panties down to rest just below my buttocks, and ran his tongue along my closed fold. I opened my legs slightly, wanting and needing to feel his tongue on my clit. *Just a little more...* He smirked and let out a low chuckle.

"Damn, baby, you're soaked." He stared at my pussy like it was his last supper, and then finally he pressed his firm tongue down onto the center of my clit, making swirls with his tongue, and hittin' all the best nerves that I didn't even know existed. My heart was beatin' so fast and so hard, that I thought it might just give up and stop right then.

"So close, Greyson. So close," I moaned, shifting my hips into his face, embracing the waves that were crashing through my body.

And then...he stopped.

"What the?"

"Say it, Vaeda. Tell me you still love me, baby girl." *Oh God, not this. I'm about to cum!*

"I – I –" My orgasm was on the verge of spilling over, and I couldn't hold it in any longer. I needed him to lick me just one more time to give me that relief that I hadn't known I so strongly craved. Just. One. More. Lick.

"I still love you, Greyson. Only you. Forever." I panted, my chest rising and falling rapidly with every breath I took, as he pressed his tongue back down onto my clit and slid his middle finger deep inside of my entrance, working my g-spot while flicking his tongue on my sensitive bundle of nerves. I came crashing so hard that I didn't know which way was up or down. I felt like I was fallin' from the sky, and he continued to work his tongue and finger the entire time until I came down from my orgasm. *Holy. Fuckin'. Fuck.*

But he wasn't finished. He undid his belt, and before I knew it, his long, hard cock was freed from his jeans, and he lowered himself onto me, pressing the tip into my opening. I was on birth control, so I didn't have to worry about getting' pregnant again, thank God. The pressure from his thickness felt so good. He pressed himself fully inside of me, and I was so wet from my orgasm that he slid in and out easily, but I was still tight enough that I felt every inch of him. He grabbed the back of my neck, and fisted his hand in my hair. I rocked my hips into him taking all that he was giving and loving every second of it.

He picked up speed, pumping so fast in and out of me that I could feel my body tensing up and preparing for a second release. He pressed his mouth down onto mine, and our tongues danced together in perfect synchrony. The salt from his mouth tasted so good, and his lips felt like home. He took himself completely out of me, before slamming it in once more, so good and so hard that it sent fireworks through both of our bodies. I fell apart right beneath him, as he held me close and moaned into my ear, coming undone right along with me.

Sex with Greyson was the single most magical thing I'd ever experienced, and I realized now, just how much I missed it. And missed him. I knew without a doubt that this, right here in his embrace was exactly where I belonged. The only question was…for how long this time?

Chapter Twenty-Two

Greyson

Then: Twenty-two years old

Things were going great again. It had been just over four months since our family had gotten back together. We were the picture of a perfect family. Vaeda and I both went to school during the day while Lennon was in daycare, and came home at night. Vaeda cooked us dinner, and we went to bed. We had a comfortable routine. I was happy. She was happy. We both had a little money saved up from our summer jobs, thought it wasn't much, and my parents had been paying for everything for us just so long as we were in school and our grades were good. It made me feel a little uneasy, having my parents supporting me, my wife, and daughter, but that was our only option right now if we wanted to spend any time with Lennon while still going to school.

But that didn't last for long. I'd come over to my parents' house to grab some things, just as I received a call from one of the scouts who had been watching me closely this season, and I was offered the opportunity of a lifetime to play with the Tennessee Titans in the upcoming fall season. I couldn't possibly put into words how ecstatic I was. It had been my dream since I was a little boy to play for the NFL. I'd shed so much literal blood, sweat, and tears for this phone call, and it was finally happening. My dreams were within reach; so fucking close I could taste it. Playing for the NFL meant that my girls and I would be set for life. No more taking handouts from my parents and being ashamed that I was the 'other' son. The one who hadn't made his dreams happen yet. I'd be lying if I said I hadn't felt extra pressure to achieve my goals ever since my fucked-up brother managed to make it big in Nashville, and having his swoony songs played all over every goddamn radio station. My mother always thought that my dreams were too far-fetched. Not attainable for me. I'd always been labeled as the 'cocky' one with far too much confidence in myself. But guess what? I was right. I made it, and I knew that I would.

I'd spent the past hours on cloud nine, until reality set in and I realized being a member of the Tennessee Titans meant that I would have to move to Nashville. I cringed at the thought of even being in the same city as my brother. But what got me more was that how would I break it to Vaeda? Would she go with me? Would she stay? Would we do long distance? A million thoughts and questions raced through my mind. I paced around the length of the living room, too fidgety and anxious to sit down. I saw my dad and Henry pull up in front of the garage and they were messing with something under the hood of Henry's truck, so I decided to bite the bullet and go out and tell them first. I was far too anxious to keep this news to myself. I needed to tell someone. I could hardly believe this was happening.

"Hey guys," I said, shoving my fists into my pockets, pretending to be interested in whatever they were looking at. I liked cars and trucks and all that, but I was more of an adrenaline junkie on the field. I needed action. Sport.

"Hey, Greyson. What's goin' on?" Henry asked, as my father walked into the garage to get more tools.

"So, I uh…I haven't told anyone yet. It kind of just happened. I plan to tell Vaeda when she gets home…" Henry stopped what he was doing and looked at me, patiently waiting for me to continue.

"I got a call from the Tennessee Titans. Offering me a spot on their team." The air between us was unexpectedly heavy. I wasn't sure what reaction I thought I was going to get from him, but I'm not sure this was it. Was he happy for me? Angry? Upset? I couldn't tell. His expression was blank and he remained silent as he took a sharp, deep breath and shifted his body so that he was standing upright with his arms folded across his chest.

"Greyson. I'm happy for you. I am. It's what you've always wanted. You know I love both you and your brother like you were one of my own. You know that, don't ya?" I nodded, swallowing hard, having a bad feeling about where this was going.

"Vaeda will be happy for you, there's no doubt about that. She isn't cruel. But I know she won't want to just pick her life up from Gator Hill and move to a different city. She has finally just made peace with Gator Hill being her home. She won't want to leave the state of Alabama. But she will for you because Vaeda has *always* sacrificed and given her all to be with you. But have you?" I waited, my breathing hitched, and I didn't know what to say back, so he continued on. "Can you ask her to, Greyson? Can you ask her to change her life for you so drastically, with all that's happened? Will it be good for her and her history of depression? For the baby?" Fuck. This is exactly what I was afraid of...

"What do I do, Henry? What choice do I have?" Henry shook his head, knowing this wasn't an easy decision. It wasn't that simple. It was messy and complicated like my life. Damned if I do and damned if I don't.

"You kids are still just that. Kids. You're so young. You both have full lives ahead of you still. Vaeda hasn't had an easy upbringing. Her world was turned upside down at just six years old. You know that. Then you two brought a baby into the mix. I love that baby like she was my own, too. But Vaeda needs to finish school, and focus on herself and Lennon. She's always done right by you, and now it's your turn to do right by her. You know what I mean, son?" I did. I hated it. I knew what was right for Vaeda, but it fucking killed me to do it. I've been selfish my entire life. But now I really had to be selfish, and to follow my dreams without her. I needed to do this on my own, and let her find her own path in life.

"Fuck!" I shouted into thin air, cocking my fist back, and letting it slam into nothing. I didn't want to hurt her. But any way this went down, she would end up getting hurt. There was no way around it. Despite the heavy weight sitting on my chest, telling me I was going to regret this, I knew what needed to be done. I had to do what was best for *her* and for our daughter and for myself. Maybe someday, down the road things could be different. But for now, this is what it was and what it had to be. This was my lifelong dream; the chance of a lifetime. My one and only shot at financial freedom and to make sure my daughter never went without. But I had to do this alone. No matter how much it killed me. I was doing this for us. Wasn't I?

Chapter Twenty-Three

Vaeda

Then: Twenty-one years old

"You're lyin'! Oh my God, Greyson that's great! This is what you've always wanted!" This was not what I was expectin' to hear when I came home with Lennon from visiting Dotty and Uncle Henry, but holy smokes, this was great news! I knew one day he would make it big. We all did. Greyson was confident and never for a second doubted his ability, and a lot of people, includin' me, used to think he was pompous and cocky as hell because of it. But there was no denying his natural talent with football. He'd broken numerous records in high school, and was easily always the best on the team, even from day one in elementary school when he played for the Little Gators. Dotty always said she thought he was born with a football in his hands, because growin' up, he always had a ball clutched under his arm. There were many times when Aunt Annette would have to make him set it down for dinner, and even when he did, he always had to keep lookin' at it to make sure it was still where he put it. My husband was goin' places…big places…and I couldn't be happier for him. It would mean big changes for all of us. I really wasn't ecstatic about havin' to leave Gator Hill and start over somewhere new, especially away from the only family I had. But there was no way in hell I would ever let him pass this up. We would still be able to come home and visit, and maybe we could even spend the off-season back here with our family. We'd certainly be able to afford it now. I could transfer schools and finish my degree and get a job in Tennessee. It would all work itself out as long as we had each other.

But the look in Greyson's eyes gave my stomach an uneasy, queasy feeling.

"Aren't you happy? This is what you've always wanted!"

"Yeah, no…I am. I am happy. But Vaeda…" he sighed, and ran his hand through his shaggy, blonde hair that desperately needed a barber's attention. "You're not coming." *Um…what?* I laughed, bitterly, unable to comprehend what he'd just said. Surely, he must be jokin'. Why the hell wouldn't I come?

"Shut up, Greyson. This is no time for jokes." He was joking. He had to be. That's the only thing that made sense.

"I'm serious. You and Lennon are staying here. I'll pay for the apartment and everything to keep you guys afloat while you're still in school. But Vaeda…I have to do this on my own."

"What the fuck do you mean? We're married!"

"I know. I want to stay married. But I'm not letting you uproot your comfortable life here to follow my dreams and me. I'll come home and visit whenever I can and I'll call you every day. But I'm doing this on my own." He wasn't joking. He was dead-ass serious, but why? If I said I didn't mind uprooting my life and movin' to another city to be with him, who the hell was he to tell me that I can't?

"No. I'm comin' with you. It's my decision to make. It won't be easy, but we'll make it work. We always

165

do, Greyson." I felt a sense of desperation with my plea, and I hated it. I hated being desperate, because that wasn't me. I didn't need a man to make me whole. But I loved him. We had everything together.

"Vaeda…I don't *want* you to come with me. I'm sorry. I want to do this chapter in my life alone. I love you and I know you'd follow me to the end of the world, but…"

"But fuckin' what, Greyson? What the hell did you even marry me for then?! Huh?!" My mind was spinning in circles and my chest felt like it was being weighed down by a thousand pound bowling ball. Was he seriously doin' this to me again? Was he seriously leavin' me? After everything we'd been through?

"I wanted to do the right thing. I wanted Lennon to have a father. And she will…she'll always have me."

"Oh, you just wanted to do the right thing, huh? So what about me? What about *us?!*" I felt the tears fighting to spill from my eyes, and I fought like hell to keep them put. But it was no use…I was bein' abandoned again by the boy who swore he never wanted to hurt me, but kept doin' just that time after time again. I couldn't believe what I was hearing. What he was saying! He only married me to do right by the baby, who wasn't even fucking biologically his!

"I'm tellin' you what, Greyson. If you leave this house without me, I will never forgive you. I will never take you back. Ever!" He stood up from his spot on the couch, and his face was completely expressionless. I didn't see pain in his eyes. I didn't see regret or even a glimpse of his love for me. He just walked right past me and out the front door without so much as another word. I'd like to say that things worked out in the long run. That he'd apologized and told me he wanted me to come with him. To be a family no matter where in the world we were. But that simply was not the case. There was no happy ending for Greyson and Vaeda; the one and only boy who ever held my heart would forever destroy me. How very stupid I had been to let him back into my life, only to build me up and tear me back down again. He was good at that. Destroying me.

Chapter Twenty-Four

Vaeda

Then: Twenty-two years old

Another Christmas had come and gone without Greyson here with us. It was especially hard last year. It didn't feel like Christmas at all without him here to complete our family and watch Lennon tear into her gifts. I had to try and be strong for her to give her the magical Christmas she deserved. This year was a bit better. Maybe because I was bitter instead of heartbroken. Greyson had come home for two weeks before Christmas but said he had to get back for training. I'd be lyin' if I said I wasn't relieved for him to leave and for our lives to go back to normal. I'd finally adapted to a new routine without him here, with school, work, and daycare. There were no fights and no tears. When he came home this time, things were just different. He'd kept a lock on his phone and always

168

placed it face down, which was the first red flag. I tried to look at it once just out of curiosity, because we were still married after all, but I couldn't get in it without his passcode. I'd tried his birthday, Lennon's, and mine; none of them worked. I still wanted to keep my family together, but I was just so angry still at how everythin' went down. He. Left. Me. I would have gone with him. I would have followed him to the end of the world if it meant we could be together. I wasn't heartless; I was happy he was living his lifelong dream. But he'd chosen to take on a responsibility that wasn't even his and then married me. Marriage means commitment. So what was he hiding? Marriage means sacrifice. So why wouldn't he get over himself and let me go with him? Marriage means love, but that was the furthest thing from what I felt for him right now. I didn't want to throw in the towel just yet, but damn it was hard not to. Maybe this time apart would actually be good for us. One could only hope.

It was five o'clock on Christmas night, and Lennon and I were over at Dotty's for Christmas dinner. She always made a ginormous spread and had Aunt Annette and Uncle Reed over for supper.

I took my seat at the table next to Lennon, and the aroma of the apple honey glazed ham filled my nostrils, and I suddenly realized how famished I was. There were twice baked potatoes, yams, green bean casserole, whipped fruit salad, and fresh homemade biscuits with maple butter. Dotty made the entire meal herself, and wouldn't let Aunt Annette or I lift a finger. I was definitely spoiled when it came to Dotty, and I realized then just how much I missed livin' at home with them.

"My Lord, it's a miracle you've managed to stay so thin living here with a cook like this," Aunt Annette said to Calista, who brushed it off and scooped a heapin' serving of yams onto her plate. At fifteen years old, Calista was more beautiful than ever, and looked far beyond her age. Her hair was bright blonde, and her skin was porcelain without a single blemish. She'd recently begun wearing makeup, not that she needed it, but she definitely looked like a princess each and every time I saw her.

Just as I finished cuttin' Lennon's meat, we heard a knock on the front door.

"That's odd, we weren't expecting anyone else, were we?" Dotty asked, and placed her folded napkin from her lap onto the table, as she rose to answer the door.

"No, not that I know of," Aunt Annette answered her question. I didn't hear any voices from the doorway, so I assumed everythin' was okay, and I began fixin' my own plate. Until Dotty came back into the kitchen with the one person I had least expected to see standing there beside her. He wore a shabby leather jacket and a white undershirt that was unbuttoned at the collar and exposed his blonde chest hair. His jeans were ripped and his hair was shoulder length and looked clean but tangled. After I finally peeled my gaze from him, I looked over to Dotty who was still standing beside him, and her eyes were filled with fresh tears.

"Shay?" Calista was the first to speak. Not even Aunt Annette or Uncle Reed knew what to think or say. I could tell by their shocked expressions that neither of them knew he was coming here. Shamus' eyes locked with

171

Calista's, and she rose from her seat at the table and gave him a long hug that almost made me feel uncomfortable. They'd always been very close since the first day she came to live with us at just three years old, but he hadn't been home in such a long time. More than four years.

"My God it's a Christmas miracle," Aunt Annette said, through tears of her own. She was the next to rise and hug her son. Uncle Reed remained planted in his seat, and the look on his face told me that he wasn't happy to see him. Not like this. He looked run down and unwell, and I felt physically ill just lookin' at him. I had to get out of here. Now.

I pushed out my chair, just when my phone started ringing on the table, and before I could even see who it was Lennon had taken it upon herself to answer.

"Daddyyyy!" she squealed, causin' all heads to turn to her. Even Shamus'. The look in his eyes was one of pure shock, and I don't know what else. But I didn't like it one bit. I didn't want him to look at my daughter. The one he'd run out on and abandoned, and left for his own brother to raise as his own. What kind of man was he? I panicked

172

when I saw that Greyson was on FaceTime. I tried to take the phone from Lennon and take it outside or in another room at least, but she pulled the phone away from me.

"Lennon, give me the phone!" I yelled, snatchin' it out of her small hands. Shamus and the others chatted amongst themselves in the background, and suddenly Greyson's face looked grim.

"Who is that?" he asked as I tried to make my way around the table.

"What?" I pretended not to hear him.

"Merry Christmas, brother," Shamus said, puttin' his face right next to mine on the camera.

"What the fuck?" Greyson spat, and I hung up feeling nothing but pure panic.

"Vaeda…Hi," Shamus said, causin' the bile to creep up the back of my throat and burn my esophagus.

"Lennon, honey, come on, we'll take your food to go. Mommy's not feelin' well. My stomach is just off." I didn't know what else to say or do, but I knew one thing for sure that I sure as shit was not spendin' Christmas eating dinner with Shamus Tucker. I wanted to hit him. I wanted to scream. I wanted to take his balls in the palm of my hand and squeeze until he couldn't reproduce another human being to walk out on. But here and now was not the time or place for it. Nobody obliged as I gathered up Lennon's plate and placed tin foil over the top of it and left. Part of me wondered if deep down they all knew what had transpired between us, but I didn't care. Lennon had no idea who he was, and I planned on keeping it that way.

"Mommy, who was that man who showed up to dinner?" Lennon asked innocently from the back seat.

"I'm not sure, honey. I've never seen him before." I felt guilty for lying to my daughter, but what the hell else was I supposed to do? She was only three years old! There were pictures of him everywhere at her grandparents' house, but the man who showed up today didn't look anything like the man in those photos. He was completely unrecognizable. I wasn't sure if it was the drugs or the booze or the tireless hours spent rehearsing his music, paired with lack of sleep, but he looked grossly unwell.

"Can I call daddy back, pwease?" Lennon asked, snappin' me away from my thoughts. Her face looked so innocent and my heart broke for her and I felt every bit as guilty as I did angry.

"In a while. You know what? I think the diner is open. Let's go have supper there, yeah?" She nodded, contently, and I sighed, takin' a left turn toward Winston's Diner where I still worked part-time.

Our bellies were full and my heart was heavy as I climbed into bed that night. I clutched onto the bear my father had given me when I was a child, and let the tears fall freely down my cheeks. I hated feelin' like this. I hated that Shamus was Lennon's biological father. I hated that he just showed up here out of nowhere and ruined our Christmas. I hated that Greyson wasn't here. I hated that I was spendin' Christmas alone in my bed and I didn't have my parents to turn to when I needed them so badly. I really fuckin' hated that Rufus wasn't hear to lay his furry head on my lap and let me know I wasn't alone and that everythin' was gonna be okay. I hated all of this.

The tears were never ending and I licked the salty drops off from my lips and let myself really feel the pain. It took a lot for me to break down and cry, but when I did, it was like a hurricane of tears and emotions that completely took over my body and left me panting and feeling exhausted and numb when the storm was finally over.

I saw the light from the hallway creep into my room as the door opened, and I saw a figure standin' over my bed. I shot up in a panic, my heart drumming hard in my chest.

"Vaeda."

"Greyson? What are you doin' here?" Startled, I quickly turned on the lamp on my bedside table, and looked at him. He looked just as distraught as I did. Except, he hadn't been cryin'. His face was hard and angry, and his eyes were wild and dark.

"Where is he, Vaeda?" I knew he was talkin' about Shamus. But did he think that he was here? That I'd brought him back here and shacked up with him or something?

"I don't know. I left as soon as he got there. I had no idea he was even coming."

"Vaeda, listen to me…you need to stay the hell away from him. He isn't well. He's on drugs and he has been for a long time."

"Okay, why are you tellin' me? I don't want anythin' to do with him."

"Good."

"Did you drive all the way back here on Christmas night just to make sure he wasn't in my bed?" He scoffed as he took a single stride over to the edge of my bed and sat down. This was my bed. We didn't share it. When he came home from time to time to visit, he always slept on the couch. We didn't touch. We barely even talked. It was like living with a complete stranger and not the only man who'd once been my entire world and been my first for everything. My first and only love.

"No. I wanted to make sure he wasn't trying to see Lennon. Did he talk to her?" I shook my head, and wiped the last of my tears away from my cheek.

"You've been crying."

"What do you expect, Greyson? This isn't how I'd imagined my life. Raisin' my daughter completely alone while goin' through school while my husband is in another city…another state…"

"Doing what?" he interjected. "What is it that you think I'm doing, huh?" He was getting defensive, and I wasn't in any mood to have this conversation right now.

"It's late and I'm tired."

"Do you think I'm cheating on you? Is that it?" I snorted in response, because it was quite obvious that he was. I wasn't born yesterday.

"I'm not stupid, Greyson. I know you haven't been faithful to me."

Just then, right on cue, his phone rang and I stood up to peek at who it was once he pulled it out of his jeans pocket, just to validate my suspicions, and sure enough, the name Rachel Barnes flashed across the screen.

"Exactly. So get the fuck out and let me go to bed." Un – fuckin' – believable he was. Why the hell did he even insist on being married? We weren't married in any sense of the word, but only on paper. I was sick of it. On Monday before class, I was making a pit stop at the courthouse to file the paperwork for a damn divorce. And I did. Only I didn't know then that this would be far from the end.

Chapter Twenty-Five

Greyson

Then: Twenty-four years old

"Ayyyyyy you the man, brotha! That play was the shit, and that pass...man, you got an arm!" Lucas Jay said, as he slapped me twice hard on the back. We'd just played and won our very first game of the season. The fans were cheering loud, and the girls in the stands were going wild. *For me.* I live for this shit. This feeling. The intensity. No matter how many games I've played, I never get tired of the game or the fame.

"Thanks man, you really stepped up tonight too." And he did. Lucas was our newest member on the team, and although he was a rookie, he had a hell of an arm on him. I was sure he was going to be an asset to the team.

"Well, I practice with the best," he said, giving me a playful punch on the arm.

Just then, I heard a low whistle come from Lucas' lips, the kind of whistle you make when you see someone really attractive. I looked around to see what hottie Lucas was onto now, when I was smacked in the face with the image of my fucking wife.

"Hot damn, I don't usually go for the brunettes, but she is fiiiiiine! Finer than fine actually, she's…"

"My wife, so how about you shut your mouth before I shove your own dick up your ass."

"What? You have a wife? Since when?!" Clearly this kid did not read the tabloids or watch much T.V. Every time I was caught talking to a girl after a game or even grabbing something to eat having meaningless conversation with a woman, the media painted me out to be some kind of womanizer who didn't give a fuck about his family.

"Vaeda," I breathed, ignoring Lucas' annoying slew of questions. I think he got the hint because he walked away and was now talking to some of the other teammates.

"Nice game," she said, pursing her plump lips together.

"Thanks. Where's Lennon?" I had no idea she was coming here. I hadn't seen her in months outside of FaceTiming with Lennon. She'd been avoiding me since Christmas time when she had me served with divorce papers. I drove my angry ass right back to Gator Hill and we had it out. I made it crystal fucking clear that I was not now or ever going to divorce her. I wasn't psychotic by any means. If I thought that was really what she wanted, then I would give it to her. But it wasn't. I knew it deep in my heart. I felt it in every part of my soul. In my bones. I knew she didn't want a divorce, and I sure as shit didn't either. She loved me and I loved her, and all we needed was to just find our way back to each other somehow. But how? So much has happened. She was so distant. All she did was push me away. I know that I'm the one who drove that wedge between us on purpose to protect her. I kept her in Gator Hill because I know that's where she belongs. With her family and familiarity. I didn't want her following my dreams and me. She needed to make her own dreams come true in Gator Hill. But if she wanted to keep this game going, then I would play it. But I was going to play it my way. I would fucking win. *Or so I thought…*

"Dotty asked to keep Lennon for the weekend. They were goin' to some bake show in Gavenport." She shifted and folded her arms across her chest. Was she uncomfortable? She looked beautiful as ever wearing a blue jean jacket over a flowing white blouse that hung just low enough to where I could admire her bulging cleavage. Her ebony curls rolled loosely down her back. But what really caught my attention was the tiny silver hoop that hung from her nose.

"You pierced your nose?" I questioned, surprised. She shrugged her shoulders as if it were no big deal. It wasn't, except she knew how much I hated all that extra garbage. She didn't need it. Makeup, high heels, piercings, revealing clothing…she was so naturally beautiful in every aspect of the word that I'd always just wanted her to see it. To know it.

"My friend Juliet did it."

"Juliet?" I hadn't heard her ever mention a Juliet before, and I found myself wondering how much I'd actually missed since I'd been away.

"Yeah, we met when I visited Sunnyside for the summer and she actually goes to the same school as me." I nodded, taking it all in. Her voice. Her appearance. *Her.*

"So why'd you come?" I asked, swallowing the frog in my throat.

"To be supportive as a friend. I was lonely without Lennon and wanted to keep busy."

"A friend, huh? I thought she was your wife?" Lucas interrupted, walking over to us with a couple of the other guys trailing behind him.

"We're not…we're…we're separated," Vaeda stammered, causing the blood in my veins to boil.

"Well then, I'm Lucas. You coming to the after party?"

"Vaeda," she answered, taking his extended hand to shake. "What party?" Lucas looked smugly from Vaeda and then to me.

"At your *ex-husband's* house. He always has the best parties, isn't that right Greyson?" I liked Lucas. I did. He was a good teammate and never caused any trouble. He stayed out of my way and always did as he was told. But he was really barking up the wrong fucking tree if he thought that…

"I'll be there then." Vaeda flashed him a girlish smile, as he looked her up and down, taking her in with his eyes. Making me want to lay his ass out right here on the field.

"Hey you! You did great out there," Rachel Barnes said as she jogged up the field to me and rested an elbow on my shoulder. Rachel was one of our cheerleaders and she was a good friend to many of the teammates. She reminded me a lot of Harper Lennox – blonde, thin, tan, and a huge chest. But Rachel was different. She was materialistic as all hell and cared way too much about her appearance and what people thought of her, but she actually had a good heart. She was caring and she'd do anything for anyone. Especially me.

"Hey, I'm Rachel," she introduced herself to Vaeda, who was still chatting with Lucas and kept glaring at us out of the corner of her eye. She was trying to be discreet I could tell, but I still saw it.

"Vaeda," she replied, sharply before walking off with Lucas and the other guys. "I'll see you at the party!" she hollered over her shoulder at me.

"Yeah. I guess so."

When I got back to the house I rented out, there were already several cars parked outside and people wandering around the back deck by the pool with their cups. My eyes darted around scanning the crowd for one face and one face only.

"There you are," Rachel said, jogging up to me just like before. I smiled at her presence, and unlocked the back door to pour myself something strong. I wasn't much of a drinker these days. A couple beers every now and again, but I liked to be in control. I didn't want anything getting in the way of my game or clouding my judgment. Many times I didn't drink at all during my own parties. I just watched over everyone else in their sloppy, drunken state. But tonight was different. Vaeda was here and I was already on edge. I needed a drink, just one, to slow the fire raging inside of me.

Everyone seemed to be enjoying themselves and getting lost in the music that blared through my Bluetooth speaker. They helped themselves to drinks and snacks that I always so graciously provided to anyone over twenty-one. I didn't allow minors at my parties. I took enough headlines and front covers of the tabloids. If it wasn't me, it was my brother, but fuck if I'm going to think about him tonight. Tonight I needed to relax. Let loose and have fun. I'd been training hard as fuck for months now preparing for tonight's game.

I reached down and unlocked the cupboard where I kept my personal secret stash of booze for rare occasions when I actually wanted a drink, and grasped the bottle of tequila in my hand. Jose Cuervo. I poured a hefty amount of the contents into a glass and tipped my head back, letting the cool liquid swirl around in my mouth, savoring the flavor, before letting it burn all the way down my throat.

"Ahhh," I breathed out just when my eyes met the pair of baby blues I'd been looking for. She was standing in the living room talking to Lucas and some of the other teammates, but she didn't seem to look too interested in whatever they were talking about. She appeared to be relieved when our gazes met, and she offered a small smile before strolling over to where I was standing at the bar.

"Nice party," she said, taking it all in with her gorgeous eyes, before locking eyes with the bottle of Jose Cuervo and visibly cringed.

"I guess," I replied, casually with a shrug of my shoulders. "Don't like tequila?" I asked.

"Not my cup of tea."

"He giving you any trouble?" I asked, nodding my head in the direction of Lucas.

"Luke? Oh no, he's fine. He's sweet."

"*Luke?*" I repeated. I'd never heard anyone call him that before. *Sweet? I don't fucking think so.*

"Mhmm. He seems like he means well." *Is she trying to test me?*

"Right, well you're still married, so there goes that," I replied, taking another swig of my drink.

"We're separated, Greyson."

"Yeah, well…it is what it is, I guess." I didn't know why I said that, but nothing new there. My mouth moves far quicker than my brain, as usual. She jerked back by my response, no doubt as shocked as I was by what I'd said. I didn't mean to act so nonchalant about our situation, but she knew how I felt. I don't need to spell it out for her again just to get rejected. Talk about slap in the face.

"Well, I should go. I just wanted to support you."

"You can't go so soon, Darlin', you practically just got here," Lucas yet again interrupted, placing his hand on the small of her back and pulling her alongside of him as he strolled off toward the pool.

"Mother fucking fucker," I mumbled to myself, as I tipped the last of the smooth liquor down my throat.

"You know, you're cute without the potty mouth. But when you talk like that you're hot as *fuck*," Rachel purred into my ear, once again coming out of fucking nowhere. I scoffed at her statement, and the lack of sense that it really made. She was terrible at flirting and I'd be lying if I said this was the first time she's tried it.

"You really need to work on your pick-up lines, Rachel."

"Why, it's working isn't it?" she smiled girlishly, resting her chin on my shoulder.

"No, Rachel, it isn't. I'm married. And she," I nodded toward Vaeda who was still deep in nauseating conversation with Lucas. "Is my wife."

"I know. But she doesn't seem to care," she said, seeming pleased that Vaeda and Lucas were chitchatting up a storm.

"Well, I do. And whether we're together or not, I'm unavailable."

"Whatever you say, Greyson. But just know when you catch her screwing Lucas later, you know where to find me." She danced her fingers along the side of my neck and shoulder before walking away, no doubt to throw herself at one of the other guys.

Chapter Twenty-Six

Vaeda

Then: Twenty-three years old

I found myself actually missing Greyson with the more time passed. I don't know why, I just did. I tried to fight like hell and reason with myself that he was no good for me, and I think it worked. But I still missed him. It was the start of football season, and everyone in Gator Hill was going crazy, all of them rooting for their hometown football star, Greyson Tucker. I was never huge into football, although I did watch it from time to time with Uncle Henry, and I knew all the basics. I'd be lying if I said I'd watched a single one of Greyson's games. Not in person. Not on T.V. Not even a little snippet of a video on YouTube. Nada. But for some reason, I decided I really wanted to watch him play again. To support him as the father of my child. Nothin' else, of course. I always loved watchin' him play when we were kids. He was a natural.

I took a deep breath in and out before dialing up Dotty.

"Hi honey," Dotty answered, and I could hear the smile in her voice. She always loved when I called, and I tried to as much as possible. We were still very close despite my busy schedule these days.

"Dotty…I was wonderin' if…if maybe…"

"Oh dear," she sighed, and I could tell I was worrying her.

"No, it's nothin' bad. I was just wonderin' if maybe you could take Lennon for the night so I could go watch Greyson's first game?"

"Oh," she giggled softly, but I could tell she was holding her hand over the receiver so that I wouldn't hear her.

"Of course, I will! But don't you have to order your ticket way in advance?" she asked, making a good point.

"I'm his wife. I can get in. Trust me," I said, sounding more confident than I felt.

"Well, sure I'll take her, and you can go enjoy yourself. I'm heading to a bake show this weekend in Gavenport, and she can go with me. The others will love her!"

"Thank you Dotty, you're the best."

***

As I figured, I had no problem getting into the game. I told them who I was, showed them my I.D. and the poor guy looked at me like I was a beaten, lost puppy. Surely, he knew who I was from the tabloids that never painted a pretty picture for Greyson. Nobody could ever say anything bad about his skills, but boy did they sure have a field day with his personal life. Greyson was frequently called a cheater and scorned for abandoning his family...their words not mine. He was seen frequently having dinner with other women, especially one in particular, the little blonde who was hanging from his neck right now.

LOVE YOU MOST

I was about as interested in Lucas as I was Caleb Streeter all the times he'd thrown himself at me. But Greyson didn't need to know that. Lucas was in fact, really nice and damn good lookin' too. I had to sit back and watch Greyson flirt with dozens of girls throughout the years; danglin' them right in front of my face. So now it was his turn to sit back and watch.

I'd be lyin' if I said I had paid attention to a damn thing Lucas was ramblin' on about. Mostly himself, I think. Figures. I pretended to be interested, tossing my head back and laughing every now and again just to appear engaged.

I immediately recognized the tiny little blonde who was following Greyson around all night, from the tabloids. Her name was Rachel Barnes, and I quickly put two and two together from Christmas night when her name popped up onto his phone. I wasn't stupid. I knew there was somethin' goin' on between the two of them. It didn't bother me anymore. He needed to live his life and be happy, and so did I.

I only had one drink, but I was pretty tired and ready to take off for the night and go back to my hotel room, when I decided to look for Greyson to say goodbye. I'd called for a cab and they would be here any minute, but Greyson was nowhere to be found.

"Whatcha lookin' for, Darlin'?" Lucas asked, makin' the hairs on the back of my neck stand up. Everywhere I turned, there he was like an annoying' little spider that just appeared out of nowhere and wouldn't go away.

"Um, I'm just lookin' for Greyson. I'm about to head out," I said, opening and closing random doors without any luck.

"Ah, I think I saw him go this way. Come on, I'll show you," he said, as he led me by the arm down a narrow, dimly lit hallway. He opened up a door that was lit from a lamp in the far corner of the room that was spacious and immaculate with a king sized bed right in the center of the room holdin' no one other than my mother fuckin' husband with Rachel Barnes. Greyson was sittin' on the edge of the bed with his head down, and Rachel appeared to be comforting him with her arms wrapped tightly around his broad shoulders. They both jumped at the sound of the door opening, and Greyson looked entirely guilty, while Rachel looked pleased.

"My bad, man, I didn't know the room was occupied. We were just…yeah," Lucas stammered, completely taking me by surprise. What the hell was he talking about? He told me he was taking me to find Greyson. What the hell was goin' on?

"Real fuckin' nice, Greyson," I said, and quickly turned on my heel to leave.

"Vaeda, wait!" he yelled, but it was no use. I wasn't staying at that party for one second longer. It was a mistake to even come to begin with. I should have never come here, and I should have never even bothered to show my support at his game. It clearly went unnoticed and unappreciated like most things with him.

I stormed out of the party like a bat out of hell and thank God my cab was already outside waiting', and I told the driver to get me back to my hotel as fast as possible. With every mile that separated Greyson and I, I felt a sense of peace yet loneliness come over me. It was the weirdest thing. He was a dick. An Asshole. A bully. A cheater. He was clearly moving on and I should too. So why the hell did it hurt so bad? I wanted this separation. I wanted a divorce. I wanted this all to be over and done with for good. *Didn't I?*

***

"How was she?" I asked Dotty, as I hugged my girl as tight as I could manage through the throbbing in my chest. The warmth of her body and the beat of her heart resonated with mine, and it made me feel better. I fought back tears most of the drive home this mornin' and I thought for sure I was gonna cave and let loose a time or two.

"Oh Vaeda, thank you for coming to see me. And you brought little Lenny with you. Come give your ol' Aunt Dot a hug, yeah?" Dotty asked, and I let out a deep throaty laugh. Uncle Henry's humor must have been rubbin' off on her since I've been gone. It felt good to laugh, and I needed it badly, until somethin' in Dotty's face told me that she wasn't joking. She looked utterly confused.

"Did she behave alright?" I asked, ignoring her odd statement.

"Did who behave alright, dear?" she cocked her head to the side and her older blue eyes were squinted and filled with question.

"Dotty, are you alright?"

"I think…I think…Oh, you mean, Lennon. Yes, of course, she was a doll. She's always a doll, aren't ya Lenny?" she asked, smiling warmly at the scared child who was clinging tightly to my jeans.

I felt oddly unsettled on the drive back home. I couldn't help but feel that somethin' was off with Dotty. For a while now, she'd forget simple things here and there and blame it on her age. She was beginning to actually appear much older than she really was; her hair rapidly greying and she was forming some ridges on the sides of her eyes. My heart panged as I pushed away thoughts that maybe something was really wrong with her. There couldn't be though. She couldn't possibly have…no, she was far too young for that. People don't lose their minds until they're much, much older. Except being in medical school, I sadly learned that sometimes that simply was not always the case.

As I lay in bed that night, tossin' and turnin' the tears that I'd been holding back and fighting like hell to keep away, had won. They made slow streams down my freshly moisturized cheeks at first, and the next thing I knew, I was balled up on my bed rockin' back and forth. I hated when this happened. When my unshed tears would build up and come pouring outta me all at once. When my pain masked by bravery would unveil itself and show its true colors in the simplest yet most painful way. My tears betrayed me, yet again.

As I caught my breath and tried to steady my rapid breathing, my phone rang next to me on the bed. I lifted it up, squinting my eyes from the excessive brightness, only to see that it was the only name that made my heart skip a beat when it flashed across my screen.

"What?" I answered, tryin' my hardest to sound casual.

"Finally! I've been calling you all day. Wait…are you crying?"

"No, go away, what do you want?!" I groaned, hatin' how vulnerable I suddenly felt.

"I wanted a chance to explain," he said, breathing out heavily.

"I don't wanna hear it, Greyson, I really don't."

"Listen, I know how it looked. I do. But I swear to you I was only in my room to get away for a minute. I was upset, and…"

"And what, you found comfort in Rachel?" He was silent on the other end, and I knew he knew he fucked up.

"No. I didn't. I swear. She followed me in there; she must have seen me walk away. I saw you with Lucas and…"

"And what, Greyson?! I'm not like you. It literally pained me to talk to him; he's so damn arrogant. Oh wait, he reminds me of someone else I know."

"So you weren't…you know, into him or whatever?" he mumbled, and my cheeks betrayed me by forming the slightest smile. *He was jealous.*

"What? No! God, no. There hasn't been anyone else for me, Greyson. *You're* the one with the lock on your phone and being caught with other women day in and day out, *not me*." I heard a long sigh on the other end, and I knew he knew I was right. It would have been too much to ask to be a normal family. To be wherever my husband was. For him to be faithful to me and love me like he promised he would. But sadly, that was not the case. All he ever proved to be was the cocky star quarterback, chick magnet...Greyson. Asshole. Tucker.

Chapter Twenty-Seven

Vaeda

Present day

I couldn't sleep last night, even if I had tried. I didn't...try. I had far too much on my mind. Within the last week, Dotty seemed to spiral downward at an alarming rate, and much quicker than any of us ever thought. It was tough to watch, but it was even tougher to know that our time was gettin' closer to say goodbye. I wasn't sure if it was easier or harder being able to say goodbye to the ones you love. I didn't get the chance with my parents or with Lennon. They had both taken me by surprise and flipped my whole world upside down. I got to say goodbye to Rufus, and for that I guess, I was glad. I needed him to know that as much as it killed me that it was okay to go. I would be okay, and that I would see him again someday. I was there with him until he took his very last breath and I wasn't goin' anywhere, but he was goin' somewhere far better than here. A single tear trickled down my cheek as I thought of him now, and how very different it would be to say goodbye to Dotty. Rufus was my dog, my pet, and my very best friend for many years. But Dotty was my aunt, my blood, my family, and the *only* family I had left.

Is it better or worse to know the one you love would leave this earth and your life forever? I wasn't sure. But I would soon find out.

A loud, steady knock sounded at my front door, and my heart clenched at the knowledge of whom it was. I hadn't talked to him at all this past week. I knew he was planning on comin' up and that he wanted to 'talk'. But he hadn't called and I hadn't put forth the effort either. The energy shifted all around me, and it was almost as if I could feel him before I even opened the door. The air felt thick and heavy and every nerve ending on my body was heightened. I had to try extra hard to breathe.

I twisted the brass knob of the door and opened it wide, our eyes connecting in ways that they hadn't in so many years. I heard myself gasp in response to my own body, and I internally kicked myself in the ass for having such an obvious reaction to the mere sight of him. But his presence quite literally took my breath away. I wasn't sure how after all these years and after all the pain, the hurt, and the suffering that he'd put me through, how one man alone could still appear *that* damn attractive to me. His hair was styled in the usual shaggy blonde do, hangin' just over his eyebrows. He was dressed in a nice light blue button down, rolled at the sleeves, and the color was identical to his eyes, makin' them pop and stand out more than ever. His faded blue jeans hugged all the right places, and his thighs looked toned and strong. His lips…*oh God, those lips.*

"It's nice to know I have the same affect on you as you do me," he rasped, huskily, his voice sending a shiver all down my back.

"What do you mean?" I asked, playin' dumb, though it was of no use. He knew as well as I did the undeniable connection we've always shared since we were young and tried to fight it off with our endless bickering and pranks.

"Trust me...I felt it too," he replied smugly, sidesteppin' me and walkin' through the door.

"Lennon's not here," I blurted out in a panic. He turned to look at me, his blonde brow raised in question.

"I know. She's at a friend's house. I told you I was stopping by...remember?"

"Um...yeah...I...I said to call first." His lips tugged into a small smile, revealin' his top row of teeth that were immaculately white.

"Sorry. Forgot. I uh...I wanted to talk to you about us, but then everything happened and I figured we should start there. I'm surprised you haven't ripped my head off already. I wouldn't blame ya if ya did."

"What are you talkin' about?" I questioned, following him into the living room and ploppin' myself down on the ottoman opposite him in the love seat. He cocked his head to the side and pinched his brow together.

"Have you been on social media today? Watched the news...?"

"Um…no, not really. My mind has been…occupied to say the least." He nodded slowly, before bringing his fist to his mouth and baring his teeth down on his knuckles.

"What the hell is wrong?" I asked, unable to stand the anticipation of whatever he was talkin' about.

"Oh boy…" he sighed heavily, and dug his phone out of his pocket and scrolled with his thumb before standing up and striding over to me to show me his phone. I took it from him and right there in front of my face read the words:

"FOOTBALL STAR, GREYSON TUCKER, KNOCKS UP ONE-NIGHT-STAND AND PAYS HER TO KEEP SILENT."

Greyson Tucker, star quarterback of the Tennessee Titans, has allegedly impregnated one of his *many* one-night-stands. Rachel Barnes, a Titans cheerleader, has come forth to talk about her time spent with Tucker, and just *how much* he paid her off to keep silent. He does have a wife and daughter at home, though you would never know it by the

**amount of time he spends with various females
around Nashville. He doesn't seem camera-shy when
it comes to being photographed with these women,
so why all the hush-hush now? Clink the link below
to watch the full interview.**

My heart was in my stomach. I couldn't breathe. I
couldn't think. I couldn't talk. I couldn't react. I felt...I
don't even know if I felt anythin' other than completely and
utterly...*numb.* Of all the lies, the hurt, the betrayal...this
has surely taken the cake. This far surpassed anything he'd
ever done before. And what's worse...I was now a
laughing target in my hometown. There was nothin' *hush-
hush* about our very separate lives. Everyone knew
everything about us since he was in the spotlight. And now
everyone would be laughin' at me more than they already
were.

"Vaeda..."

"Don't! Don't you dare fuckin' say my name." The
anger and hurt in my tone was obvious. He'd done it yet
again.

"Vaeda, it's not true! You have to believe me! I've never…I would never…"

"You would never *what* Greyson?! Get her pregnant on purpose?! Well that's what the fuck happens when you stick your *dick* in someone without protection, *moron!"* I spewed.

"Oh, cuz you're one to talk!" he scoffed, disgustedly. *Was he fuckin' serious right now? He can't be serious…*but he was.

"Do you have any idea how much you've embarrassed me?! I can't even walk down the road without people starin' and whisperin'! What the hell do you think they're gonna do now, hmm?"

"That's what you care about? Seriously? What people *think* of you?"

"Wouldn't you?!" I shot back.

"Do you not know me at all, Vaeda? After all these years, you really don't know me, do you?" I could see the hurt written all over his face, and it pained me to look at him and see it, but no amount of pain he was feeling could ever compare to the daggers in my own heart.

"We never will have our happily ever after will we? It's just not in the damn cards for us is it?" I asked sadly, more to myself than to him.

"I'm requesting that she get a paternity test done," he said, as if that changes things. As if it changed the fact that he'd been unfaithful to me for all these years. It didn't. It didn't change a damn thing. I hoped for his sake and for Lennon's, that he wasn't the father. But for me, it didn't matter. Our story ended a long time ago, and I was just too stupid not to see it. Despite the animosity between us, I was still hopeful in the back of my mind that things would eventually turn out okay between us. That Vaeda and Greyson would find their way back to one another the way we always had. Throughout all the bullying, the fighting, the tears, and the hate that our love would come out even stronger. But I was wrong. I was so very wrong.

Chapter Twenty-Eight

Greyson

Present day

Despite all that was going on with the media and me right now, I still wanted to go and visit Dotty. Who knows if there would ever be another chance to see her and talk to her. She was a huge part of my life since I was in diapers, always dealing with my wild ass, more than my parents ever did, and I owed it to her to be there.

My parents had already heard the news by the time I'd gotten to their house. I could see it on their faces. They tried to play it off like they didn't know, because I think they wanted to hear it from me first, but they'd never been good at hiding their feelings. I think my father truly believed that it wasn't my baby. My mom on the other hand…I don't know what the hell it would take for her to ever believe in any good coming from me. She agreed that I should get a test done and then we would go from there. I already knew without a doubt what the results would be. It would change everything.

My phone was ringing off the hook all morning long, but I hadn't answered a single call. I hadn't even reached out to Rachel yet. Part of me was actually really shocked that she would have gone to the media with something like this. She'd always come across as really caring and charismatic with a heart of gold. I think that's why most of the team had her on their side. I didn't. I didn't want any part of that despite her efforts. She was a piece of pussy for the team to pass around, and in my eyes, she was nothing more. No matter how hard she tried.

"You know, Greyson, it's a shame that you haven't been by to see Dotty a single time in the past year and a half that she's been here," my mom said as we pulled into the parking lot of the residential facility.

"She knows how busy my life is, Mom," I expressed bitingly, not in the mood for her guilt trips right now.

"Does she though?" she asked, bitterly.

211

"Annette," my father warned, always hating family confrontation. He never tolerated my brother or I to disrespect my mother, not that I ever wanted to, but sometimes it was just so hard. She knew just how to get under my skin and to make me feel less than worthy. Just like someone else I knew.

"Hi Stella, how are you today?" my mom asked, as Dotty's roommate answered the door with a bright smile on her face.

"Oh, I'm better now that's for darn sure," Stella said, sounding amazed as she looked me up and down, causing my father and I to exchange glances, and I couldn't help but let out a chuckle. Nonetheless, it lightened the mood.

"Nice to meet you. I'm Greyson," I offered as I held my hand out for her to shake.

"I'm Stella and I'm twenty-one," she joked with a wink.

"Oh, you old bat, don't you be bothering my guests," Dotty said, slapping her friend playfully on the arm.

"Greyson," Dotty said, taking me by the arm and pulling me into a tight hug. She hadn't seen me in years and she still knew exactly who I was. It melted my heart into a puddle right at my damn feet.

"Dotty, I've missed you," I said, and I did. I thought of her every single day. My second mother.

"I've missed you. My how you've grown. Look at those muscles, boy!" she exclaimed, pinching my bicep.

"Yeah," I chuckled. "Comes with the job, I guess."

My parents and I chatted with Dotty and Stella for a while, just catching up. It was great to see her, although admittedly it was a little different not having delicious food shoved down my throat. I definitely missed that. I felt terrible that literally the one and only thing she loved to do, cook and bake, was something she wasn't ever going to be able to do again. I couldn't imagine being stuck in a place like this at just sixty-something years old, and never being able to throw a football again. The one thing I loved to do. My life might as well just end at that point because football is a part of me; it's who I am. Just like being in the kitchen is who Dotty is.

213

Suddenly, I had an idea. A brilliant fucking idea. It probably wouldn't work. It would most likely just be a waste of time, but I at least had to try.

I cleared my throat as I stood up from the wooden chair that I'd been sitting in next to the others.

"Could you guys excuse me for a minute? I need to go outside and make a phone call." Nobody seemed to mind, aside from Stella, who grabbed my bicep once more and squeezed it, before I walked out of the room and into the hallway by the nurses' station.

"Excuse me," I said to a younger looking nurse, who couldn't have been more than twenty. She had bright blonde hair, fake no doubt, and her eyelashes were so long they touched her eyebrows when she blinked. I couldn't help but wonder how in the world that didn't tickle.

"Oh, um, uh hi," she stammered, her cheeks flushing to a deep pink. "What can I do you for? I mean, I just meant, um." Watching her struggle to form words was just as painful as it had to be for her to talk. It physically pained me to see the struggle on her face, as well as watching her eyelashes comb her brows. I just couldn't take another second of it.

"I'm Greyson Tucker," I extended my hand to the young nurse. "I'm here visiting Dotty Cooper." Her face lit up at the mention of Dotty, and I was instantly relieved and a tad bit hopeful.

"She's…she's like a mother to me, and always has been. I know it's been really hard on her being here…in a place like this, only in her sixties." She nodded her head as I talked, so I decided to just bite the bullet and dive in.

"She's a really good cook. Like *really* good. Cooking, baking…you give her a kitchen and she'll give you the best damn meal you've ever had." The tiny nurse cocked her head to the side, and I was sure I'd lost her.

"I'm sorry, I don't…I don't follow." I sighed, becoming slightly annoyed.

"Look. She's wasting away in here. As I'm sure most of these old folks are. But Dotty, she's…she's not that old. I know she's unhappy, and she's going to die. It's inevitable. We can't change that. But we can help make her last days, weeks, months, however the hell long she has here a little bit happier."

"And what exactly are you proposing that we do?" she asked, arching her back slightly so that her breasts perked up in her too-tight scrub top. I internally rolled my eyes at the gesture, but I needed to work with it.

"I'm asking you," I began, taking a step closer to her and lowering my voice to my most charming, convincing tone. "To let her help cook for the residents. Everyone here gets fed three meals a day, and there's no one who knows how to throw down in the kitchen like Dotty does, believe me."

"I'm sure she's amazing, Mr. Tucker, but I'm sorry, that's just not something we've ever had happen here. I mean we have a cook. We don't just let the residents back in the kitchen, doing God knows what, while half the time they're not in their right mind." I knew she had a point. I knew that was probably what she was going to say. Which left only one thing left to do...

I grabbed her small hands and held them into mine. A gesture that quite literally meant nothing to me, but I knew how to get what I wanted, and I could feel her tense up at my touch. My eyes darted to her nametag, and quickly back to meet hers.

"Trina...please. I don't expect you to let her back in the kitchen if she's not in her right mind, but I know there are times when she knows what is going on. Like right now. She's herself, she's normal as could be, and yet, I can tell she's unhappy. Sad. No life left in her. I've known her my whole life. It's what she loves. Who wants to live a life without passion? Without doing what sets your soul on fire," I said, bringing her hand up to my heart for good measure.

"Okay," she jerked her hand out of my embrace, and shook it off. She took a deep breath, and my heart sped up with the anticipation. I really wanted this for Dotty. I don't know why, but I just did.

"Okay, I'll talk to my boss." My heart sank at the realization that Trina didn't actually have much say in the matter, and I realized I'd wasted all my effort in trying to half-ass flirt my way into getting what I wanted.

"My mom's my boss," she added, after my face fell. "She won't have a problem with it." I took a deep sigh of relief, and instantly felt my tensed muscles calm. "But for the record. I don't fuck with married men," she said, her eyes darting to the white gold band on my ring finger. I'd never taken it off. Never wanted to. Not that it'd ever stopped any women before from hitting on me, and I found myself a little surprised that Trina had noticed, let alone cared. I smiled a boyish grin, knowing full well she caught on to what I was doing.

"Your schmoozing might have worked this time, but seriously, you need to work on your sincerity. I could tell you were about as interested in me as you are ol' Beverly over there," she said, nodding to an elderly resident in the corner who was passed out in her wheelchair with drool running down the side of her face.

"I'm sorry," I said, admittedly a little embarrassed. "It's just…she's important to me."

"Yeah, you said that. I'll make it happen. But seriously…go home to your wife," she replied, taking me by surprise. *If only it were that easy…*

Chapter Twenty-Nine

Vaeda

Present day

I couldn't help but be miserable as all hell after Greyson dropped the bomb on me like that yesterday. A baby?! Are you fuckin' kidding me? Of all the shit he's put me through over the years, this by far was the most surprising. I guess somewhere deep down; I always thought or at least hoped that maybe some small, tiny part of him actually did love me. Like really, truly loved me. I mean, how could he not after all we'd been through together? But I was a damn fool. A total fuckin' idiot. He didn't love me, and maybe he never did. He loved the chase of havin' to work for me. He loved torturing me. He loved belittling me, and making me feel like I was nothin'. He loved takin' my first kiss. My virginity. Takin' every damn part of me, until I felt like I was nothing. Worth nothing. But I swore to myself that this was the last straw. The nail in the coffin. The final act that really did us in for good. I would do whatever I had to do to get him to sign those divorce papers, even if it killed me. I needed to finally be free of him and move on with my life for good.

"What's bothering you dear?" Dotty asked, taking me away from my thoughts.

"Oh, nothin' Dotty. Just thinkin' is all."

"About Greyson?" she asked, makin' my body tense up.

"No. Why would you think it's about Greyson?"

"Because you get this look about you when you're thinkin' about him. This glare in your eyes and your cheeks flush just a smidge. Maybe not noticeable to some, but I raised you, ya know."

"I know," I answered, feelin' slightly guilty for lyin' to her. "It's just – he really messed up this time, Dotty. I thought it was over between us, ya know? I thought I didn't care anymore."

"Sweetheart, whatever that boy has gone and did now must've hurt you pretty badly. I can see it in your eyes. But one thing I know for sure, is that even when he tries to be all hard and mighty, there's an even bigger part of him that is just as sweet and soft and tender as can be. I've always seen both sides of him, the good and the bad, fighting one another. Years ago, he'd pull some God-awful prank on you and make ya cry, but as soon as he saw your tears and knew he'd actually hurt you, he'd turn right around and run off. Found him cryin' a couple times too after hurtin' your feelings.

"You did?" I didn't know that. It took a lot to make me cry, but of course Greyson Asshole Tucker would be the one to make it happen. But him? He didn't cry. Not in front of me anyway. He always appeared so tough and unbreakable on the outside.

"Mhmm." Dotty took my hands in hers and I looked into her sad eyes.

"As much as you think he loves hurting you, I know for a fact that he doesn't. It hurts him just as much if not more to see you hurting. But it's always been his way of getting your attention. Have you ever heard the saying, negative attention is better than no attention at all?" I nodded.

"That saying is for kids who act out with their parents to get their attention, Dotty."

"But it's the same with Greyson. I remember when y'all were kids. Babies even. You wouldn't give him the time of day. You paid him no mind at all, although I could always see you watchin' him from afar. But if he even came near you, your defenses immediately went up and you'd push him away. So he saw what it did to you and how you reacted, and he went with it. It was the way you communicated with one another. I remember when you were just four years old. Your mama had brought you over and y'all spent the weekend with us. We went out back to let you kids run around in the sprinkler. Well, there was a snake over near the garden. Greyson told you to watch out because you were runnin' around barefoot, and he didn't want you to step on it. You ignored him, and I think you might've told him to piss off or something of the sort," Dotty chuckled and I thought back to the vague, but familiar memory.

"Well, he got so upset that he picked that snake right up by its tail and chased you around with it. He was grounded for quite some time for it, but it sure as heck got your attention."

"The snake bit me," I whispered, starting to remember that day so long ago. Dotty pursed her lips and nodded.

"He was so distraught. After your mama fixed you all up and put you to bed, Greyson was nowhere to be found. We searched for a good half an hour or better, and finally when we found him, he was down by the river bawling his eyes out." I shot my head up, confused.

"The river down the road from your house?" But when he saw me ride my bike down there so many years ago, he acted as if he'd never seen it before. That place was my sanctuary for so many years. The place that Lennon and I used to go to escape; to be alone and just swim and get away for while. The place I lost my virginity. The place where everything changed between us. All along, he'd known of it, but maybe his memory blocked it off because it was painful for him. That was the day we had our very

223

first fight. Where our mutual hate for each other truly began.

"Mhmm." I sighed heavily, not knowing what to even say. I wanted to tell her what was going on with Greyson and the pregnancy scandal right now, but she didn't need any more on her plate. Who knows how long she had until she lost her memory again, and I didn't want to waste precious moments dwelling on negativity.

"I love you, Dotty. You know that, right? You've always been so good to me. One thing is for sure, and that's that I will take your wisdom with me wherever I go in life. Whether it's with or without Greyson Tucker."

What happens when the one person you hate more than anything, becomes the one person you can't live without?

Chapter Thirty

Greyson

Present day

I decided to stay in Gator Hill for a while longer than originally planned. I didn't feel like putting up with the media, and being followed by reporters trying to get me to talk. But that plan backfired when someone snapped a picture of me leaving my apartment in Gator Hill and uploaded it to Instagram, and now I had dozens of reporters waiting outside my building, just waiting for me to talk. It wasn't going to happen. I had nothing to say. I took the paternity test a few days ago, and was still waiting to hear back on the results. I knew what they would be. I wasn't a fool.

Vaeda hadn't spoken to me since a week ago when I broke the news to her about the scandal. She told my mom she didn't want Lennon coming over until everything settled down. I couldn't blame her, but I couldn't stand not seeing my daughter either. She was the only reason I even had a separate apartment in Gator Hill.

I still hadn't spoken to Rachel. I would only be fueling the fire when all I really wanted to do was put it out entirely. I needed everything to go back to normal as soon as possible. I really needed to talk to Vaeda. I tried calling her several times over the last couple of days, but to no avail.

I paced around my house, contemplating what to do, when my phone rang in my back pocket. It was a Private Caller, which I normally wouldn't have answered, but I wanted to just in case it was someone calling on the results of my paternity test. As luck would have it, it was.

I could barely hear the voice on the other end of the receiver, as I so stupidly peeked my head out the curtain topper placed on the window of my front door.

"Greyson!"

"Mr. Tucker!"

"Mr. Tucker, what does your wife think about the baby?! Is she going to stay with you?"

Despite my conscience telling me it wasn't a good idea, I just knew what I had to do. Adrenaline was pumping through my veins and it was clouding my judgment. I shoved my phone back into my back pocket and opened the front door to take it all in. Fuck if I cared about what they thought or had to say, but if Vaeda wouldn't answer my calls, this would surely do the trick. The reporters went wild when I walked out the door and locked it behind me. Half of them froze up and looked so surprised that I even walked out the door that I think one of them even had piss running down their leg.

"Greyson!"

"Greyson, are you going to get a divorce?"

"Greyson, why did you pay her off? Did she take the money?" I cleared my throat and raised my hand in the air to signal them to shut the fuck up.

"Excuse me! Not that it's any of your damn business, but I would like to clear the air for one person and one person only. My wife." My eyes locked on the camera and microphone that was immediately placed in front of my face. "I just got the call that the paternity test is

NEGATIVE and will be followed up in writing. But of course, I already knew that because I never once slept with Rachel Barnes. Never even laid a finger on her. She's nobody to me. Nothing. The only one who matters to me…the only one who has *ever* mattered to me is my wife. Vaeda Clarke. The love of my life. Vaeda, I hope you see this and that you find comfort in knowing that I would never deceive you. Never cheat on you. You're it for me, Vaeda. Only you. Only. Ever. You." And with that, I turned around and smiled the widest smile I'd had in days, and pulled my pants down to moon the motherfuckers before I ran off to my car and sped away.

It only took a matter of three minutes before my phone went crazy with phone calls, and I realized they wasted no time uploading the video of my speech to the web. Due to the nudity, the video was reported and taken down on several sites, but it was of no use, it'd already gone viral.

I took a left turn toward Vaeda's house just as I clicked on the video and heard my voice playing back to me. It was epic. Legendary. And *damn,* I had a nice ass.

I chuckled to myself as I looked up at the road, the adrenaline still in full swing. But when I did, I saw nothing but black.

Chapter Thirty-One

Vaeda

Present day

I'd like to say I was shocked by the video, but it was so Greyson. He fuckin' mooned the cameramen and his ass was everywhere on every social media platform. There were already several memes floatin' around making light of the situation. I can't say I wasn't happy to hear that the DNA results were negative. But for him to say he never cheated on me? Never deceived me? That was a fuckin' lie, and he knew it. He had girls of all ages, shapes, and sizes wrapped around his finger, and he loved every bit of the attention they gave. That's always how he was. An arrogant son-of-a–

"Shit!" I yelled, as I realized I was bein' paged from the hospital. I'd started my internship a few weeks ago, and I was never happier to be in the line of work I was in. St.

Paul's was the number one hospital in Alabama, and its fast paced environment was right up my alley. I felt like I was in an episode of Grey's Anatomy every time I worked. I loved every minute of it. I got to assist on the most bizarre operations, from operating on someone who got a hairbrush stuck in their rear end, to a woman who swallowed her wedding ring because her ex-husband asked for it back to give to the her sister.

I couldn't imagine what I was bein' paged into now. Hopefully somethin' good.

"What do we have, Dr. Dole?" I asked Shayna, the attending I was assigned to for the week.

"Um, you mean you haven't heard?" Lucy, one of the interns chimed in, while Shayna paid little to no attention to me as she was frantically goin' through a stack of papers.

"Um no?" I responded to Lucy. Her hands were clutched tightly to my arm, as if we were besties walkin' through the middle school hallway to art class.

"It's basically God himself! Or a country God, rather. Except God wouldn't drive drunk to the point where he hit another car head on and put himself in a coma with numerous breaks and contusions to his pretty little, literal definition of perfect –"

"Lucy! Enough already, God, you're giving me a migraine and we haven't even stepped foot into the OR yet!" Shayna yelled, causin' us both to flinch. "I'm gonna need more coffee for this one, while they finish prepping the OR." Shayna walked away with an empty coffee cup in-hand, and for some reason, nothin' was makin' sense to me. Maybe I just didn't want it to. Maybe I didn't want to know. Or maybe I already did know, but my mind and body couldn't connect to really comprehend the situation.

"It's *The Heartthrob!*" Lucy whisper-yelled into my ear. All of a sudden, my legs went completely numb. I had no idea how I was still standing. It was hard to breath. My lungs felt incredibly heavy, and it felt like I couldn't get a good deep breath. Shamus? What? How? When? What the...

"It's all set, you're in OR two. Hurry, it's pretty bad. Where's Dr. Dole?" one of the nurses asked.

"I'm right here, let's go Vaeda and Lucy, you're with me! Get scrubbed in." I wasn't sure if I should have been operating on him. My brother-in-law and the biological father of my child. To be honest, I'd never mentioned my connection to the famous *Shay Tucker* before. Here, in this hospital, I was more than just Greyson Tucker's estranged wife. I'd never legally took his last name, because I never really got around to filing the paperwork, but then once things went south, I decided I'd be better off. I was right. At St. Paul's Hospital, I was Dr. Clarke, a surgical intern who graduated at the top of her class. I was good at what I did, and everything I did, I did it with precision, passion, and fire.

Part of me wanted to explain that I couldn't operate on this man lying before me with a face so dang bloody that he was pretty much unrecognizable. Yet, a part of me knew that I needed to save him. As much as I hated him, and even with as much time that went by that he had never known his…my…*our* daughter…I knew my job was to save lives. His life was no different from the rest.

"Jesus," Shayla muttered, beneath her mask. "How many DUI's does a man have to get before they put their keys away when they're tipping the bottle?"

"Was he drunk?" I asked, curiously, trying my hardest to concentrate on the procedure before me. We were operating on his brain, performing a complex craniotomy. The scans showed that Shamus had an aneurysm for quite some time, which the accident caused it to burst. A clip needed to be placed over the base of the aneurysm. It was an incredibly diverse procedure, one I'd never observed before. Luckily, I was mostly observing and barely assisting.

"How did he not know he had an aneurysm?" Lucy asked, as my eyes remained glued to the opening of his brain. Never did I think I would see the inside of Shamus' body. It was scary, and it wasn't at all as cool as it was on other patients. It really hit differently when you knew the person lying on the table in front of you.

"Drug use, I would presume," Shayna answered casually, as if she saw this type of thing every day. The bile stung the back of my throat and I had to fight to regain my composure and hold it together. Had he really been that strung out? Did he really have an actual problem? I knew he dabbled and experimented with drugs. I assume it came along with being in the music industry. But I guess I just didn't know things were this severe. And driving drunk? How could he have been so careless with not only his life, but also everyone else's?

I took a deep breath as I watched multiple hands moving a mile a minute and I actually wondered for a moment if I could do this for the rest of my life. Have someone else's life quite literally in my hands. One wrong move, and they're dead. My heart sped up and I could feel a surge of panic come over me. *Breathe Vaeda, just breathe. It's just your anxiety talking. You're fine. You were born for this. You've never wanted to be anything but a surgeon a day in your life.*

"Clarke!" Dr. Dole yelled so loud it made me flinch, and I snapped out of my thoughts. "Did you see what I just did? If you don't pay attention, you can get the hell out of my OR!"

"Um, yeah. Sorry. It's just. I just that know him is all. It's just gettin' to me a little bit."

"Yeah? We all know him, and if you don't snap the hell out of it, he's going to just be somebody you used to know. Now do what I just showed you."

"What? By myself?" I had yet to assist in the procedure, and neither had Lucy, and she looked just as stunned as me.

"Um, yeah. Can you handle it, Dr. Clarke? Or do you need to assist the ER with putting Band-Aids on scrapes and stitches?"

"I am more than capable of doing my job, Dr. Dole, but I just…I've never…"

"Well, this is how you learn. Take the scalpel." I swallowed hard, and tried my hardest to mimic what I saw her do a minute ago. My hands were shaky and my heart was pumping in overdrive, and I couldn't believe that I was about to operate on Shamus Tucker.

BEEP! BEEP! BEEP!

"His pressure's dropping, what are you going to do, Dr. Clarke?" Shayna shouted at me, testing me. How could she be testing me at a time like this? She should just do it herself! *No. I can do this. I've been trained for this.* I squeezed my eyes shut for a moment, as I had no time to waste. I inhaled through my nose as deeply as my lungs would allow, and exhaled all of my doubt, nerves, and every negative thought. Every bad thing Shamus had ever done in life to me and everyone else was out the window, just like that. Now it was time to save his goddamn life.

***

I managed to remain as calm as possible as I completed my portion of the procedure and continued to assist throughout the remainder of the surgery. For some reason, Lucy wasn't even asked to assist with stitching him up, despite her several attempts to be hands-on. Shayna shut her down and told her she was strictly just observing. We were both interns and I thought of her as my equal. She always made intelligent decisions and I thought she was precise with her work. Although I was confused as hell as to why I was the only one allowed to assist, I was grateful for the opportunity, no matter how scary it was or how close to home it hit.

"Good job in there, Clarke," Shayna said to me as we cleaned ourselves up.

"Thanks. Why…why did…" I began.

"Because you're a natural. You are capable. There are a million other surgeons in the world just as good as you, don't let it get to your head. But I saw how hesitant you were in there. Lucy? She didn't even bat an eye. She was ready to do whatever it took to complete that procedure, and that's what a good surgeon does. I didn't choose you because I thought you were better than her or any other doctor in this building. I chose you to show you that you can handle it. Don't ever question your capability. This isn't the line of work for it. If you want to be scared, if you want to be hesitant, if you want to choke up…go sit behind a desk, because medicine? Surgery? It's the hardest job in the world, and it's the most rewarding. You don't have time to second guess yourself when someone's life is in your hands, Dr. Clarke."

"Understood," was all I could manage to say. I normally didn't take shit from anyone that's just how I was. If someone mouthed off to me, I would normally give it right back. But she was right. Every word she said was right. I had to be on my game every single step of the way or I would never make it as a surgeon or in life in general. I needed to stop second-guessing my choices and myself. I needed to get out of my own damn head.

"Hey, I don't mean to interrupt, but your husband was brought in a little while ago, and he's asking for you," Lucy said, walking over to Shayna and I.

"What? My husband?" I asked, utterly confused. Lucy pointed across the hall to the room he was in, and I rushed in before my hands were even dry.

"What the hell happened?" I asked, breathlessly, lookin' from Greyson to Dr. Johnson and back to Greyson. Dr. Steven Johnson was the head of orthopedics, and he was checking over Greyson's leg, which was bleeding profusely.

"I fucked up," he said, through clenched teeth, no doubt in a great deal of pain.

240

"What in the world is going on today? First…nevermind." I realized I was about to say that I'd just operated on his brother, but then realized I would have been breaking doctor patient confidentiality.

"Yeah, I already know, it was Shamus," Greyson said with his head bowed.

"What happened?" I repeated walkin' over to the opposite side of the bed that Dr. Johnson was on.

"He was drunk, what do you think? He hit me hcad on!"

"But…you said you screwed up."

"I…I don't know. Just forget it, my football career is probably over, and I'm going to be royally fucked."

"I wouldn't say that, Mr. Tucker, but it does appear that you have a break and a small fracture in your tibia. We'll need to operate, but if all goes to plan, you should have a full recovery in three to six months," Dr. Johnson said, looking at the scans one of the interns brought in.

"Months? Jesus, just kill me now."

"Greyson, it's not the end of the world. It's off-season anyway."

"Just go. Please." I arched my eyebrow, and folded my arms across my chest.

"Go? You asked for me and now you want me to go?"

"I asked for my wife, but I forgot I didn't have one," he scoffed. Dr. Johnson cleared his throat uncomfortably, and on cue, he exited the room to give us a minute.

"Wow, okay. So we're back to that again, huh?"

"Back to what?"

"Back to you pushin' me away. Back to square one."

"Look Vaeda, you've made it very clear that you see no future for us. I shouldn't have asked for you. Just please…go." For once in my life, I didn't have anythin' to say back. He was right. I didn't see a future for us. The future I once had pipe-dreamed up was just a foggy memory of a fairytale. So I did what he asked me to do. I did what Greyson always does best. I turned on my heel and left.

Chapter Thirty-Two

Greyson

Present day

Just my fucking luck. For three to six months, I was out of commission. No training, no working out, and no football. I might as well have just died in the accident, though I hated to admit it, I knew I was overreacting. It could've been a lot worse than it was, and I'm lucky I walked away...well not really, with just a broken leg and some minor cuts and bruises. My brother on the other hand was in a coma. I asked one of the nurses how he was doing, not that I really cared, but I was just curious. The accident was his fault. He was drunk, and they'd proved it by the blood work. When the hell wasn't he drunk or high?

I hated to be the one to have to call my parents and tell them the news. I hated upsetting my parents, although it seems it happened more often than not. If it wasn't me it was Shamus, and if it wasn't Shamus it was me. Although I had to admit, he definitely had me beat by a landslide if it were a competition of who could be the bigger fuck-up. I don't even want to know what the hell he was doing back here in Gator Hill. What the hell were the chances of all the cars on the road that he could've crashed into that it would be mine? Just my damn luck lately.

When my parents arrived at the hospital, I watched them outside my window talking to Vaeda, who was surely giving them the low-down on my prognosis. I could tell by the look on Vaeda's face that she was upset with me. What the hell was new? I sat up in my bed, groaning from the discomfort in my leg. Whatever medication they gave me was starting to wear off. I braced myself for my parents to come in, carrying on about what happened, when…they walked away. Where the hell did they go?

"They went to the ICU to see your brother," Vaeda said, popping her head in the door. I nodded in response. Of course they did. I couldn't really be mad, he was in worse shape than I was in, but they could have at least said hello since they were right outside my room. *Figures.*

Hours had passed, and I was still waiting to be taken in for surgery. They wouldn't give me anything else for the pain until I was out, and I was growing more miserable and uncomfortable by the minute. I pulled out my phone to occupy myself when my door opened and my mother walked through the door.

"Hey, there," she said, as if it were a casual visit.

"Hi, Mom."

"Your brother's awake," she said, taking me by surprise.

"Oh. That's good," I replied, half-heartedly.

"He's asking to see you." I hooded my gaze, and for some reason, my heart picked up speed, and I broke out in a sweat.

"What for?" I asked, shakily.

"Greyson…he's your brother."

"Since when? When has he ever been a brother to me, Mom?" What the hell could he possibly want to say to me?

"Since you were just a few days old, and I brought you home from a family who wanted nothing to do with

245

you." Her statement made me jerk back from the rawness of her words.

"Wow. Thanks for that."

"Greyson, it's true and you know it's true. You need to stop thinking that everyone has it out for you. Not everyone was placed on this earth with the sole purpose of trying to hurt you." *If she only knew*...I chuckled bitterly, and shook my head with disbelief.

"Mom, you know nothing about me, so please don't pretend. You haven't tried to know me in years." She cocked her head to the side, as if she were clueless, but then her eyes met mine, and what I saw, was a moment of…truth.

"I know. You're right. You're very right. When I left your father all those years ago, I came home and just hoped that things would go back to normal. I tried. I did try and you know it. But I guess I could've tried harder. I buried myself with my work…I nodded, for once agreeing with something that she said.

"I know you think…that you've always thought…that I think Shamus is more my son than you are.

But that's not true. You are *my* son. My boy. My everything. Blood or not, you're my world. Just like Lennon is to you." I jerked my head up, completely floored by what she'd just revealed that she knew. She *knew*.

"How long? How long have you known?" I asked, almost breathless. Her revelation quite literally knocked the wind right out of me.

"Since the moment I first laid eyes on her. I'm your mother, Greyson, and I'm Shamus' mother too. It doesn't take x-ray vision to see that he's a part of her. Yes, she looks a lot like Vaeda, but...she is so much like him."

"No! She is nothing like him!"

"Honey..." her expression softened, and she swept a strand of dark hair behind her ear. "He's made some mistakes. Some *big* mistakes. But he will always be your brother. And you will *always* be Lennon's dad."

"You're damn right I will." We sat in uncomfortable silence for a moment before I shot my head back up to look at her. "Does Dad know? Does everyone know?" I asked as my voice cracked.

"I don't know. I've never said a word to anyone about it. But if they're as observant as I am…then I'm sure they know." I nodded, hating every word she was saying, but at the same time, a part of me felt…relieved. I didn't like living a lie. My life has been nothing but one big fat fucking lie. I was over it. Fed up. From my adoption, to my feelings for Vaeda, to Lennon…I needed everything out in the open. I couldn't hide behind the wall I'd built any longer. Enough was enough.

***

The surgery went well, and I was still in a lot of pain. I was finally being released from the hospital, but I had one more thing I needed to do first. After my talk with my mother, my father came in, and I decided to tell him the truth about Lennon and her being Shamus' biological daughter. He didn't say that he knew, but he sure as shit didn't act surprised. It felt good to get it out in the open. I didn't like everyone thinking I was just some heartless bastard who just didn't give two shits about his own brother. *He did this. Not me.* But despite the rising rage flaring through my body, I needed to know what he had to say. He asked to see me, and I swear I wasn't going to, but a part of me was just so damn curious.

I walked into his room, not able to even look up at him. I walked straight by his bed and sat down in the wooden rocking chair in the corner. I took a deep breath, and I could feel his eyes glued right onto me.

"I didn't think you'd come," he rasped. I felt my jaw clench and my thumbs wrestled in my lap.

"I wasn't going to. Don't know why I did," I answered truthfully.

"Cuz you're my little brother," he replied, as if it were that simple. I huffed, bitterly.

"Yeah. I am your brother. But you've never been much of mine, have you?" I could feel the emotions running high, the energy in the room was intense, and my heart was jackhammering in my chest. I never thought I'd actually be having this conversation with him. I never even thought I'd ever speak to him again if I was being completely honest.

"You're right. You're completely right." I nodded, glad that he was able to admit it. "I tried to be. When we were kids…we got along great. I never had much of a knack for football, but I played with you because it's what you liked to do. I just wanted to spend time with you."

"What the hell does any of that have to do with our reality now?"

"But as you grew a bit older, you were always so hard to get along with…even for me. You treated Vaeda like dirt…"

"Don't! Don't you dare say her fucking name to me!" I spewed, saliva shooting out of my mouth like I was a wild animal.

"Okay, okay…I get it. I just…I didn't like the person you were becoming."

"So you fucked my girlfriend?!"

"Hold on a minute…y'all weren't even together. But yes…I fucked up and I know that now."

"Don't even try to tell me you didn't know we had something special, because *everyone* knew it, even when I didn't!" For the first time since I walked into the room, I lifted my head to look at him. He was nodding, taking in what I was throwing back. He looked like shit. Complete and utter shit. His hair was just past his shoulders, and it was matted and greasy. He had cuts and bruises all over his body, and he looked easily twice his age. He looked nothing like the carefree, easy going brother I grew up with.

"Jesus," I breathed out.

"Yeah…drugs will do that to you."

"Well, I'm sure you'll keep doing 'em anyways." We both stared at each other for what felt like ages. Neither of us said anything, we just…stared.

"I'm sorry, brother. I really am so very sorry…for everything." I don't know why I felt the need, but I just had to address the elephant in the room. If he wasn't going to, then I would. No matter how much it pained me to do so.

"She's perfect, you know. Absolutely fucking perfect. And you just walked away…like she meant nothing. Like you didn't give a single *fuck* that you created another life. How could you do that? I mean, how could *anyone* do that?" I asked, seriously curious. I needed to know. He bowed his head and inhaled a sharp breath, and nodded his head in defeat.

"Trust me, I've spent the last nine damn years asking myself the same question. All's I can say is…I thought I was doin' her justice by not bein' in her life. I was no father…no man…I was nothing. All I cared about was my next high. I knew you'd step up to the plate. I knew how much you loved Vaeda. How much you've always loved Vaeda. I thought I was doing the right thing."

As much as I still didn't understand his mindset, I was and always would be grateful for it, because it gave me the greatest blessing in my life, and nothing would ever change that.

"I really am sorry, Greyson. I hope that one day…that we can be brothers again." I pursed my lips together, hating what I was about to do. Kicking myself in the damn ass for it.

"I was on my phone."

"What?"

"The accident…I wasn't paying attention, because I was on my phone. I felt myself swerve into the other lane and that's when I jerked my head up and realized what was happening." I said it so fast that I don't even know if I was talking clearly, but I just needed to get it out. No more holding back. I could've sworn I saw his eyes fill with tears, but it came and went so quick that I thought maybe I was just imagining it.

"It doesn't matter. I was drinking when I shouldn't have been."

"But I could've killed you," I said, hardly able to believe that he wasn't even a little mad. He'd be charged with *another* DUI and God knows what else. He was in a coma for Christ's sake.

"You woulda been doing me a favor, brother." His words cut through my core and I instantly felt the guilt and the sadness overwhelm me that I didn't even know existed. It swept over me and completely took me by the balls and squeezed the life right outta me. Shit, I didn't even think I cared if he lived or died, but hearing him say those words made me realize just how very wrong I was.

I'd like to say that Shamus cleaned his act up after the accident, and that we all found a way to co-exist, and that we went back to being brothers again...but that's his story to tell.

Chapter Thirty-Three

Greyson

Present day

Three months had gone by since the accident. I had healed completely and was now just getting back into the swing of things as far as conditioning and getting back in shape. My life went back to normal, and I was back in Nashville coming home on the weekends to be with Lennon.

My brother was serving time in Gator Hill Correctional Facility for his fourth DUI. He'd managed to get lucky up until now, but his fame could only pull strings for so long until he needed to be held accountable for his actions.

Today was Dotty's birthday and I was headed back to Gator Hill to celebrate. She was preparing a meal for all of us, and I knew it meant a lot for her to be able to do it.

Nobody knew that I was the one who pulled some strings to make it happen. I'd been talking to my mom on the phone more frequently since the accident, and she'd said that Dotty had seemed to be in good spirits since she'd become part of the kitchen help. On her good days at least, though they were growing fewer and far between, and I could tell it was really taking a toll on my mom. They'd been best friends for most of their lives, and I couldn't help but sympathize with how she must be feeling, knowing she was losing someone that close to her.

Although Liam wasn't dying, I still knew what it felt like to lose my best friend. We hadn't spoken in years. I'd seen him out at the bar a couple months ago when I went to pick up food, and he was drunk as shit, falling all over the place. I didn't even recognize him. We locked eyes, but neither of us said a single word. Not one. It was like a knife straight to the heart. But there was nothing I could do. He was still grieving the loss of his fiancé, and no one or anything could ever bring her back.

As far as other relationships in my life went, my mom and I were on fairly good terms. My parents were doing well, and I was really happy for them. I'd never be able to forget what she'd put our family through, but I found it in my heart to really truly forgive her. If she was happy and my father was happy, then that's all that mattered, I guess.

I still hadn't spoken to Shamus, but at least we laid everything out on the table. It was a start. If it never went further than that, then so be it, but it still felt damn good to get it off of my chest.

Things had long since died down with the pregnancy scandal. I hadn't seen or heard from Rachel, and neither had the other teammates, aside from one. I guess she and Lucas were together, and they kept their relationship pretty private. Kudos to them. Good riddance.

And Vaeda? Well, Vaeda was Vaeda. She was still stubborn as hell and there was still some work that needed to be done as far as "we" went. I still needed to tell her how I felt. I needed to tell her the truth once and for all, and if she hated me afterwards, then so be it. I would agree to the divorce. But at least I would be able to say it wasn't for a lack of trying on my part.

LOVE YOU MOST

For once I was early to a birthday party. My parents were bringing Lennon, and Vaeda's car was the only one parked in the side entrance by the dining room.

I climbed out and walked through the doors of the side entrance and into the dining room, but it was empty. Nothing was set up and the dinner was supposed to start in forty-five minutes. *That's weird*, I thought.

I walked into the hallway and over to Dotty's room, whose door was closed. I heard the sound of muffled cries coming from within. Was that Vaeda? I knocked twice on the door, my heart picking up speed. What was wrong? Why was Vaeda crying? I knew that sound because it was like a broken record that played over and over again in my mind from every time I'd ever made her cry. The sound alone made me sick to my stomach. Nobody came to the door, so I decided to open it. But nothing could've prepared me for what I found on the other side. Absolutely nothing.

"Vaeda…" Vaeda was kneeling down on the side of Dotty's bed and she was stroking her hair and caressing her cheek, her own tears spilling over onto a sleeping Dotty.

"She's gone, Greyson. Just like that, she's just...*gone!*"

"What happened?" I asked, rushing over to her side. I didn't know what to do, but I knew that I needed to comfort her in any way I could. My own bile stung the back of my throat and I wanted to break down and cry right along with her, but my own pain wasn't important right now. *Her pain was.*

"She laid down for a nap, she told the nurses she was feelin' tired, and she...she just...she didn't wake up. They called me right away and I came as soon as I could. How could someone just *die* on their own damn birthday? That's so cruel!" she shouted, her voice cracking and she continued to weep.

"Oh, baby. I'm so sorry, Vaeda. I'm so fucking sorry." The site of Dotty alone was enough to haunt me for life. She looked as though she was sleeping, but there was no rising and falling of her chest. Her skin was as white as snow. No movement what so ever. She was eerily still, and although we grow up knowing that our lives will eventually result in death...it still doesn't make it any easier to understand. How a life that was so warm and kind and gentle and…everything that was *good and pure*, could just be…nothing. You lay down for a nap one day and you never wake up again. You're just *gone.* Forever. No take backs.

I found myself praying to a God that I hoped truly existed, and I begged him to let Dotty be there in Heaven. I prayed and begged that she was preparing her birthday feast for all the angels. For Vaeda's mom and dad. For Lennon. Even Doofus. I hoped she was with them and that she was happy. That's the only thing that could make this situation even a little bit better is the belief that she was truly in a better place. I'll never understand how or why someone had to get sick to die. Couldn't everyone just grow old and die of natural causes when they're a hundred years old? Why did Lennon have to get cancer and die at eighteen? Why did Dotty have to lose her mind and die at sixty-four? I'll never know the answer to either of those questions. All I could do was be here for Vaeda in any way she would let me. We would get through this. Together.

We were both so preoccupied with what had happened that we never even called my parents to let them know what was going on. Henry was the first person the nurses called, and then Vaeda. Henry never showed up until much later, as he said he didn't know if he could do it at all. He was completely beside himself, and for a man I'd known my entire life, and never once saw cry, he was the worst out of everyone. He sobbed and sobbed in a way I'd never seen anyone cry before. One thing I knew for sure was that he loved his wife with every bit of his heart. Everything he did, he did for her. He worked tireless hours seven days a week on the ranch so he could provide for his family. His wife. I'd never once seen them argue. I'd never seen them cuss at each other; the way my parents often did. I'd never seen anything but pure love and adoration for one another.

It's crazy how one day you wake up and it just seems like any other ordinary day. You have plans, you eat, shower, and go through the motions like you normally would. Then BAM, your world is flipped upside down and nothing is ever the same again. Dotty touched all of our lives in a way that would never be able to be filled by another human in our lifetime. She was a second mother to Shamus and me, and especially to Vaeda and Calista. The best aunt. A devoted wife. A friend. She was all of those things and so much more. Although my heart would hurt for a while, I knew it was different for Vaeda. She'd already experienced so much loss in her lifetime. More than I ever wanted to imagine. My pain intensified ten-fold just looking at her and seeing her completely overwhelmed with grief. It was almost more than I could bear.

My dad stayed back at the house with Lennon, while my mom came to say goodbye before they took her away. We had to clean out her belongings and decide what the hell to do with them. Henry said that he didn't want any of it. He couldn't bear to look at it. He took one look at his wife, and turned around and threw the hell up. Vaeda and my mom had to talk to him and help him gain the courage to say goodbye. Dotty didn't want a funeral or any services, which she made very clear. And although it was sad, I understood it. I never wanted anyone standing over me and mourning me like this when my time came. And I know this isn't what she would have wanted either.

"Look, Greyson," my mom said, pulling out a photo from her bedside drawer, and handed it to me. It was a photo of Vaeda on her birthday. It was her eighth birthday, the one with the slip n' slide. Vaeda was posing in her orange bikini and I was in the background just staring at her longingly like a little creep. I didn't even know this picture existed. But I definitely remembered that moment. I hated her wearing that stupid bikini. I didn't want anyone's eyes on her but mine.

"Hey, that was after you yelled at me to go change," Vaeda said, her face lighting up just a smidge.

"I don't think I knew it then, but I was just claiming what was mine," I replied.

"I'll go get some more boxes," my mom said, leaving us alone.

"What's this?" Vaeda asked, pulling out a folded up piece of paper that read V&G. She unfolded it as I peered over her shoulder. It looked crisp, as if it were just written. The page was covered in Dotty's old-fashioned handwriting, and Vaeda read it out loud, as I swallowed the giant lump in my throat. Yep, here comes the water works.

Dear Vaeda and Greyson,

Yes, both of you. I can bet a blackberry pie that you're together right now as you read this. If you're reading this, then that means that the time has come for me to dance with the angels. Please don't be upset. I'm not. I've come to terms with my illness and with my death. And although I won't physically be here with you anymore, I can promise you that I will always be here in spirit whenever you need me. We will meet again someday. I'm sure of it. But until then, you will need each other to lean on. Vaeda, before you roll your eyes and say, "I don't need no man, Dotty," just listen. You too, Greyson. You both have been through so much together. You two were running around in diapers, torturing one another. But neither of you could ever just leave the other one alone. Ever. And you know why? Underneath all the pranks, the arguing, and the bickering...you love one another. You always have. You started to figure that out years ago. But love can be scary sometimes. It is the most powerful feeling a human being can feel. Your love story is unique. I would never push either of you to be with anyone I didn't wholeheartedly believe you belonged with. You know they say everything happens for a reason. And although we never truly find out the reasons behind God's plan...I believe you, Vaeda, were sent to live with me to meet the man you're meant to be with. To meet Lennon and be the best friend she'd ever had in her life, and to have that precious baby girl. God has a plan for each and every one of us. And although my story here on earth is ending...yours has only just begun. I can honestly leave here knowing that I lived a full, happy life. I married the man of my dreams. I raised two beautiful young ladies. I am content and I am at peace. When your time does come to walk with the Lord, I want you to feel the same way I feel right now. At peace. Don't leave this earth with any regrets. Go after what you want. What you love. WHO you love. Make the best of every situation, and never take a single moment of your life for granted.

And please, look after Uncle Henry for me. He won't take this easy, but he will get through it. He's strong. You all are. I love you both with all of my *heart, and there won't be a day that goes by that I won't be smiling down on you. I can feel that it is time. I must go be with the angels now. I am tired...*

Love always,

Dotty

"Wow...That was..."

"Yeah. That was intense." Vaeda added.

"Look, there's more," I said, pointing in the drawer to the other letters neatly folded up, but with other initials on them. H, S, A&R, and C. Most likely were for Henry, Shamus, Annette & Reed, and Calista.

"She knew she was gonna die when she laid down for her nap. How crazy is that? She was just so...okay with it," Vaeda said, wiping a tear from her cheek. I nodded. It was pretty crazy, but I had to admit I agreed with everything she said in her letter. I needed it to be known.

"I'd really like to talk to you, Vaeda. Would you mind coming back to my place for a little while? I promise, it's just to talk." She looked hesitant, and I held my breath until I saw her nod her head in agreement.

"I guess it's time."

When we got back to my place, I realized this was the very first time Vaeda had ever been here. I always picked Lennon up and dropped her off. I suddenly felt a tad vulnerable having her see my place. I'd forgotten I'd kept pictures up on the walls of me and her, and some with her, Lennon, and me. I didn't want to hide when I came here. This is who I am. Where I am comfortable. My apartment in Gator Hill was so completely opposite of the one I had in Nashville. My place in Nashville was far too big for one person; it was showy and lacked any…homey feeling at all. No pictures on the walls. No good memories. It cost a fortune and I was barely ever home. But this place…it was small and comfortable and 'lived in'. There were paintings hung on the fridge made by Lennon. Her bedroom was just messy enough to know she'd been here and played hard. The cupboards were full of all of her favorite snacks, unlike my empty cupboards in Nashville that held nothing but some ant traps and dusty glasses.

"Wow, this is…different than your other apartment," Vaeda said, as if she were reading my thoughts.

"It is. It's where I feel most at home."

"So, then why did you leave?" she asked, taking a seat on the far end of the sofa. I followed her lead and sat down in the recliner adjacent to her.

"Gator Hill will always be my home, Vaeda, but Nashville…it holds my dreams. It was a once in a lifetime opportunity that has changed my life." She nodded with a small smile planted on her face, as if she really understood what I was saying.

"I know. I am really happy for you, Greyson. I am."

"Are you?" I questioned. She cocked her head to the side as if it were hard to believe.

"I am. I think life really needed to take us in different directions so that we could finally learn to let go." Her words cut me to my core and I had to readjust myself in the chair to regain my composure.

"I don't…that's not…I don't want closure, Vaeda. I want…you," I said, point blank. Take it or leave it. Now

269

was finally the time to lay everything out on the table. No more games. No more running. If she decided to walk away from this now, then so be it. I would sign the damn papers. But this time, it wouldn't be me running away. I wasn't scared anymore. I knew exactly what I wanted, and it was the woman who was sitting in front of me, looking so breathtakingly beautiful that it almost pained me to look at her. Her features were so sharp and perfect in every way; her eyes icy, but not cold, her pouty lips, and her skin the most perfect shade of cream. Her dark hair was like long strands of silk that my hands so badly wanted to lose themselves in the shiny waves.

"How can you even say that? After everythin' you've put me through?" I cleared my throat, searching for the words to say.

"You've been unfaithful to me more than you've ever been true. You've run away from me…from us more times than I care to remember. I don't even think *you* know what you want." I felt her drifting further and further away from me with each word she spoke, and I fucking hated that she felt so far away.

"That's where you're wrong, Vaeda. I haven't ever been unfaithful to you. Not once in our marriage. I've never kissed…touched…Christ, I've never even looked at another woman the way I look at you. Don't you see, Vaeda? Those pictures you found in my phone all those years ago…*I took those.* I kept them just hoping you would look through and find them. I tried to act distant, just to show you what it felt like. So that maybe…maybe you would crave my attention again the way I craved yours. I talked to other girls in public when I knew there were people around to eat that shit up. I know it's wrong. I know I shouldn't have. I didn't even think about how I could be embarrassing you. I just…I wanted you to want me the way that I wanted you. The way that I *still* want you!"

"That makes no sense, Greyson! If you supposedly wanted me so damn bad, then why the hell did you run out on me? You kept shuttin' me out! For years!" she belted, with so much emotion in her tone.

"I was scared. I was scared of losing you. Scared of something happening to you. With Colt alive and still being a threat, I couldn't risk anything happening to you or

Lennon. I would rather die being miserable and lonely than to ever watch something happen to you and knowing I could have done something to stop it. I gave in. I gave him what he wanted. But he's gone now. None of that fucking matters anymore, because if he was still here…I swear to God, Vaeda, I'd kill him my goddamn self. Nothing or no one is ever going to stand in the way of how I feel about you ever again. I was scared of hurting you, but in the end that's all I ever ended up doing. I'm so sorry for hurting you, and for pushing you away. Shutting you out. I'm so fucking sorry, Vaeda. All cards out on the table. This is how I feel. You're what I want. I'm done running. Done hiding. You're my Mutt and I'm your Greyson Asshole Tucker, and it's always been you and me against the world, baby. You. And. Me."

"Wow, have I ever told you how romantic you are?" she asked, letting out a chuckle.

"Maybe once or twice."

"So…Rachel?" she asked, looking slightly embarrassed. I shook my head.

"Never laid a finger on her. Never wanted to. You're it for me, babe. It may have taken me eighteen years to realize that I love you, and it may have taken me twenty-seven years to realize that *I belong loving you*, but I'll be damned if I spend another day fighting my feelings. I am scared. I'll probably always be scared. Scared of hurting you. Scared of not being good enough for you. I want to spend the rest of my life proving to you and to myself that I am." I breathed out a sigh of relief; feeling like a ton of bricks just fell right off from my chest. I'd spent years, maybe even my whole life fighting a connection that was just too deep to run away from. I was tired. Tired of running. Tired of fighting. Tired of spending my days going through the motions and not truly *living*.

"I mean, I understand you bein' scared. I guess. But why go to such extreme lengths of making me hate you, thinkin' you were cheating on me all this time, instead of just tellin' me how you really feel?" I shrugged my shoulders and shook my head.

"I have no real explanation for that other than when I realized you were done fighting…fighting for me…I

273

felt…lost and desperate. I spent years thinking I had the upper hand, and that I was in control of my own feelings. I realize now that that's not the case. I can't control how I feel about you. I can't control how you feel about me, and that is scary as hell. I'm not used to not being in control. However, I've come to accept that I need to be okay with that. I need to let go of the past and start living for the future."

"So, where do we go from here, Greyson?" This isn't exactly how I'd imagined this going, but my heart took the reins and next thing I knew, I was standing up from the chair and in two seconds flat I was down on one knee before my girl.

"Marry me. Again. For real this time. I meant it the first time, but we still had a lot of growing and learning to do. I'm ready now. I'm ready to give you all of me. My whole heart and nothing less because I can't imagine a life without loving you, and I don't ever want to try. You're it for me, Vaeda. You're. It." Vaeda rose from the couch and covered her trembling lips with her hands. Her eyes turned a deeper shade of blue and they filled with tears that threatened to spill over her porcelain cheeks.

"I…I've never wanted anything more than I want this life with you. Yes. So much yes!" she shouted, crying and laughing, and I stood back up and lifted her in the air and threw her over my shoulder as if she weighed nothing.

"But what about football? What about Nashville and my job here?"

"Shhh," I said, in an attempt to silence her thoughts. I didn't want to think about that right now. We would figure it out together this time.

"Vaeda, football is my life. It's a part of who I am. I love it. But I love *you more.* I love you the most, Vaeda. Everything else comes second." I plopped her down onto my bed and just stared at the beauty that lay before me. She was so fucking breathtaking, and…*so fucking mine.*

"Greyson," she panted as I lowered myself on top of her, breathing in her intoxicating scent. "There hasn't been anyone since you. It's…been so long, I don't even know if I remember how to…"

"Sshhh," I whispered into her ear. "Just let me love you, okay?" I urged. "Please, just let me love you." I lifted my head and pressed my nose to hers, and looked into her hazy eyes. She nodded, as she clutched my t-shirt and pulled it over my head. The feel of her hands grasping my back sent me into a state of pure euphoria, and I couldn't help but wonder if this were all just a dream. Was this really happening? Having her here with me in my bed…agreeing to start over. Start fresh, and to continue our story.

I planted soft kisses along the base of her neck, feeling her body tense beneath me. My hands made their way inside her tank-top and I was pleasantly surprised to find her nipples rock hard, and just waiting to be nibbled on. I kissed my way down to her breasts, and slid a nipple into my mouth, toying it gently with my teeth, triggering a whimper to escape her lips. I knew how sensitive her nipples were, and I loved the effect I was having on her pleading body. The taste and feel of her in my mouth was so intense and so incredible and I just wanted to explore every inch of her hungry flesh again as if it were for the first time. I'd waited so long for this, a fantasy I'd beat myself off to for years. My dick was rock hard in my shorts, desperately waiting to explode inside of her.

I trailed my hand down to the heat between her legs, and I could feel her wetness seeping through her panties. I rubbed my thumb over her lace panties, teasing her nub and making my way down to her hole and gently pressing inward as far as the fabric would allow.

"Greyson, please," she pleaded, arching her back off the bed.

"Please, what? What do you want, baby?"

"You. I want you. Please." And so her wish was my command. I yanked her panties down her thigh, hearing a rip, until the side string came undone.

"Whoops."

"Greyson! Those were expensive!"

"You don't need them. I plan on keeping you out of underwear for as long as it takes to make up for lost time, baby girl." I grasped her upper thighs and yanked her down to the edge of the bed, as I maneuvered myself onto my knees before her, ready to taste my favorite fucking meal. I was famished. I lifted her hood to expose her bright pink and swollen nub, and I gently blew on it, savoring the sight of her perfect, tight pussy mere inches from my face. Then I dove in and ate it like I'd been starved my whole goddamn life.

I flicked my tongue eagerly on her clit while simultaneously toying with her hole with my forefinger. I didn't press it in, although she was shifting her hips upward, begging me to. Not yet. I took a short break, just to build her up further. I spread her lips wide open and just stared at the beauty before me.

"You smell so good, Vaeda," I groaned. I peeked up at her, and I saw her cheeks flush with embarrassment, so I quickly shoved my middle finger deep inside of her, to wash it all away. She screamed, not expecting the sudden change in pace. I wiggled my finger on her sweet spot, feeling the palm of my hand growing more soaked by the second.

"No. You will come with me. Do you hear me? Do. Not. Come." She whimpered, and squeezed her eyes shut as if she were in pain.

"But I'm so close. I'm right there," she begged.

"Yeah, and I'm about to come all over my shorts just looking at your sweet pussy. So we'll come together."

"Do you have…I'm not…I'm not on anything. I haven't had a reason to be." I thought for a moment, and realized I didn't have any condoms either. Like her, I had no reason to be prepared.

"It's okay. Tell me it's okay, Vaeda, and I'll fuck you like you've never been fucked in your lifetime." Her eyes widened, and without an ounce of hesitation, she nodded her head eagerly.

"Yes. Yes, it's okay. Just please Greyson. Hurry." And without wasting another second of precious time, I slid my shorts down, and my cock sprang free. I grabbed ahold of it and guided it into her hole as I lowered myself on top of her, holding her legs high up on my shoulders the way I knew she loved. It got nice and deep that way. Her eyes rolled to the back of her head as my full length was buried inside of her.

"Oh my God," she moaned, grabbing a fistful of my hair. It wouldn't be long now. I pumped aggressively in and

279

out of her, as if my life depended on it. Now wasn't the time to make sweet love, it had been far too long for that. Right now, we both needed an intense release, and I was going to give us just that. My balls smacked against her ass with every push I gave, and I could feel them bulging and ready to explode. I pulled all the way out of her as I felt her body tense beneath mine, and I slammed it once more into her as I felt my whole world spin. I came so fucking hard right along with her that I swore I saw stars. Her body shuddered and quivered beneath me, and I didn't stop until I saw the rise and fall of her chest slow down to a steady pace.

"Greyson, that was…amazing," she said as I lowered my body down to lie beside her.

"I am so fucking in love with you, Vaeda Clarke."

Chapter Thirty-Four

Vaeda

Present day

I could hardly walk straight after the sleepless night spent with Greyson buried inside of me. His parents kept Lennon overnight and we enjoyed each other's company in a way we hadn't in a long time. It was nice being there with him. It was like a whole new side of Greyson Tucker that I'd only just met, and I was pleasantly surprised to find that it existed. I loved all sides of Greyson, the bad and the good, but I'd have to say this by far my favorite version of him.

After such a stressful day with the passing of Dotty, it was a much needed change of pace, but now it was time to get back to reality. It was far too exhausting to finish packing all of her things yesterday, so I had agreed to go back and get the rest today, before I went and picked up Lennon.

"I'm very sorry for your loss, Ms. Clarke," one of the nurses said, as I passed by the nurses' station. I smiled my thanks and continued makin' my way toward Dotty's door. It was such an odd and eerie feelin', comin' here and knowin' I wasn't gonna get to see her. When I reached her room, I knocked on the door and took a deep breath. This would be the last time I ever stepped foot in this residential facility and in this room. I took one last look around at my surroundings and then the door opened. But I was confused as all hell when I saw that it wasn't Stella who opened it. It was…Juliet Rivers.

"Juliet? What are you doing here?" I asked, cockin' my head to the side. I was sure I had the right room, I'd been comin' here for almost two years.

"Vaeda, hi!" she jumped at me and wrapped me into a hug. "I'm so sorry to hear about your aunt. She was the sweetest lady," she said, holdin' her hand to her heart. "Come in." She held the door open wider, and I took a step in the room and looked around. The only other person in here was Stella who was standing over Dotty's old bed.

"It's okay, Gram, she's in a better place now. Everything will be alright." *Gram?*

"Stella's your grandmother?" I asked, putting two and two together.

"My one and only," she smiled. "She isn't taking this the best. Her and Dotty grew really close during their time here," Juliet explained.

"Hey, Stella. Are you holdin' up alright?" I asked, walkin' over to the sweet, old lady who I was always so fond of.

"She was supposed to make pie. I hadn't had a piece of blackberry pie since 1732," Stella said in a somber tone.

"1732?" I asked, gently. "That's a long time."

"One of the nurses called and said that Gram was having a really hard time since she found out yesterday," Juliet said, her expression glum.

"She was an amazing woman, and I know how much you meant to her, Stella. She held your friendship very dear to her heart," I said to try and make her feel better. I watched a single tear fall down the poor woman's cheek, as she laid down on Dotty's bed, and began singing John Newton's *Amazing Grace*, breaking my heart a little more.

"Amaaaaaziiiiing Graaaaaace," she sang, as we both stood by and watched. The tears continued to fall down her cheeks, and I rested a hand on Juliet's back, knowin' it couldn't be easy to see her grandmother hurtin' like this.

"Amazing…" she mumbled, looking up at the ceiling. I turned to the stand that held the rest of Dotty's belongings, and tried to give them a little privacy.

"Amazing…" I piled the rest of the clutter into the box, suddenly beginning to feel overwhelmed with emotion, and just needing to get out of here as fast as possible.

"Amazing…"

"Gram are you tired?" Juliet asked, runnin' her hand through Stella's grey-white curls. What happened next knocked me. Right. On. My. Ass.

"Dotty. There you are, my friend. This is amaze…" her voice faded off into the distance, and I stood back up to see the heavy rise and fall of Stella's chest, until it…just stopped, and a soft moan escaped her lips.

"Gram? Gram, wake up! Gram!" Juliet shouted, shaking her grandmother frantically. "Gram! Gram!" Two nurses ran into the room and hovered over the bed, one consoling Juliet while the other checked Stella's pulse and confirmed that Stella was gone.

"But she was just singing! She was fine, she was singing *Amazing Grace*, and it was her favorite song! And then…and then…" Juliet broke into tears and fell to the ground at my feet, and I couldn't help but feel so deeply for her, as I knew what she was feeling all too well.

"Shhhh, it's gonna be okay," I consoled her. "She saw Dotty, didn't you hear? She saw her and they're together now."

"She's not supposed to be with Dotty, she's supposed to be with me! She's all I have left! She's all I have!" she yelled, clutching onto me like a stuffed animal, and squeezing so tightly that I swear our bodies molded into one.

"I know. I know exactly the feeling." I did. I knew exactly what it was like to lose every person you ever cared about. Every person who ever took care of you, and it wasn't easy. It never got easier, despite what people always said. It didn't get easier. The pain never went away. It just got easier to mask the feelings like a Band-Aid. The wound was always present, but the Band-Aid just helped to suppress the bleeding. Even if it was just a little bit.

***

"How is it possible that my heart can physically ache like this? I never knew what heart-broken actually felt like, or if it even had a real feeling at all. But it does. It hurts so bad, Vaeda. It hurts so damn bad," Juliet cried into my lap, as I ran my fingers through her dark hair.

"I know. I know it does." Juliet had no other family what so ever, so I offered for her to come back to my house for the night, so that she wouldn't be alone. Not only did I know exactly what she was going through, but I also felt like maybe Dotty and Stella brought us together for a reason. I've always been a firm believer that everything happens for a reason, even though most of the time I have no idea what that reason is. But I feel like her and I becoming friends…was just *meant to be.* I hadn't made a single friend since Lennon died. Not one. Acquaintances at med school and at work sure, but a real friend? No. Not even close. The truth is I didn't really want to. In some ways I almost felt that if I made a new friend, I'd be disrespecting' Lennon somehow. I know it sounds silly because I know she'd want me to have friends. I know she'd want what's best for me. I know she'd love Juliet.

They were so alike and yet so different in so many ways. They both felt everything deep in their core, sensitive and sometimes a little dramatic. It's what I loved most about them, their ability to feel so deeply. Maybe because I could see a small part of myself within them, and I've always had to act stronger than what I truly felt. Because if I didn't…I'd never make it in this life. With all of the loss

I'd experienced, I couldn't afford to fall down. If I did…I'm not sure I would be able to get back up. But Juliet showed me that it's okay to grieve. It's okay to mourn. It's all part of the healing process. If you don't hurt…if you don't grieve…then how will you really ever be able to grow? And so, for the first time since I'd left the residential facility yesterday…I broke the hell down. I cried, and sobbed even. I let myself feel everything I was tryin' my damnedest not to feel. I cried for Dotty. I cried for my mama. I cried for my daddy. I cried for Lennon. I cried for Rufus. I. Just. Fuckin'. Cried. For what felt like days. We both laid on opposite ends of the sofa and just released all of our emotions. When we were done…when I swore I didn't have another single tear in my goddamn body left to shed…then we laughed. We told each other stories of Dotty and Stella and of my mom and dad. I told her all about Lennon and even Rufus. We talked for hours until all of a sudden it was the middle of the night, and I couldn't believe time had slipped right away from us. For the first time since Lennon died…I really felt like I had a friend. Like I *could* have a friend. Someone who listens, and who cries when I cry, and who laughs when I laugh. It felt…so damn good.

"My heart doesn't hurt so bad anymore. I mean it still hurts…but it's a little easier to breathe," Juliet said, and I nodded in agreement, knowin' exactly what she meant.

"Isn't that crazy? I've heard stories about people dying from a broken heart, but I was sure it was bogus. But you know what? I think I actually believe it now. For a while there, I thought it might happen to me. I'd never felt anything like it before." Then it clicked like a light bulb that just flicked on in my head and everything began to make sense. I knew exactly what I was put on this earth to do. I was going to fix broken hearts. I was going to be a cardiothoracic surgeon. I would be the best damn heart surgeon St. Paul's had ever seen. I was sure of it.

Chapter Thirty-Five

Vaeda

One month later…

"So do you like it? Your job?" I asked Juliet, as I shoved one of Lennon's mini muffins into my mouth and chased it with a Hi-C.

"Love it. Being an alcohol and substance abuse counselor is so rewarding. I love just taking a step back and listening to other people's stories and their feelings because I can relate. I was them." I slowed my chew on my next muffin as I furrowed my brow, completely caught off guard by her confession.

"You mean…you were an addict?" I asked.

"I was. I am. I'll always be an addict, which was the hardest thing for me to come to terms with. I'll never be able to just look at a drink without downing twelve and going and picking up an eight ball. It's just not how I'm

290

wired. I had a choice. I made a choice. I made the choice to do drugs. It completely ruined my life. Now I'm just…taking my life one day at a time and thanking God each and every day that he gave me a second chance. I get to help others who wrestle with the same demons as I do." I nodded my head slowly, my thoughts taking me to Shamus and Liam. My heart hurt for the broken road they'd gone down, and I only hoped that one day they would seek help and come out on the other side like Juliet did.

"Yeah. Greyson's brother and his best friend both struggle with it too." I told her all about the history between Shamus and I, but I didn't get into detail about the path he'd chosen years ago. It was his story to tell.

"They're both pretty far gone from what Greyson's told me. I think Liam is just mostly into booze, but who knows anymore. I haven't seen him in ages." It made me sad to think about, especially when I thought about all the times we'd spent together, the four of us; Lennon, Greyson, Liam, and me. Whether we all liked it or not, we were stuck together from school, our families, Lennon and Liam bein' together, and then Greyson and I. We eventually became one big happy family…until we weren't. I missed those days when life was simpler. When all I had to worry about was whatever stunt Greyson was gonna pull at my birthday party.

"Will they be there? At the wedding?" she asked. Greyson and I had decided to get married in five months when the football season ended. We didn't want to wait too long because we were already married, but we wanted to do things the right way this time. Without any obligation, or any reason other than our love for one another. I shrugged in response to Juliet's question.

"Shamus won't be. He's in jail, and he doesn't get out for another year or so. As far as Liam goes, I don't know. I know Greyson would like him to be. I think he plans on stoppin' over and talkin' to him sometime soon. They kind of had a falling out."

Just then, the front door opened and Lennon came runnin' in full-force and jumped straight into my arms.

"Mama! Mama, guess what?!"

"What, baby?" I asked, tuckin' a strand of her silky, dark hair behind her ear.

"Daddy said he'd sign me up for singing lessons! I'm so excited! I wanna play my guitar *and* sing! Just like my Uncle Shamus! Maybe one day I can grow up to be big and famous just like him! Wouldn't that be cool, Mama? Then I could get rich and take care of you and Daddy!" Greyson stood behind her, and we made eye contact. I could see it in his eyes that this wasn't easy for him to do.

"That's great, baby! I'm so happy for you. Now go put your bag away and get washed up for dinner, okay?"

"Can I have a snack first? I'm staaaarrrrvvviiiiing!" she said, arching her back dramatically as if she were gonna faint.

"Not before dinner, Sweets."

"Why not? It looks like you ate four packages of my mini muffins," she said, holdin' up the empty wrappers as evidence.

"Did I eat four?" I asked in astonishment. Well, I'll be damned. I guess I did.

"Maybe you're pregnant," Juliet joked and winked at Greyson. Then it hit me. Greyson and I both stared at each other, all the blood draining from both of our faces.

LOVE YOU MOST

I was late.

Chapter Thirty-Six

Greyson

Present day

"Are you sure?" I asked in a state of complete shock. I definitely didn't see this coming. "We only went unprotected just that one time."

"Greyson, I'm sure. If the plus sign was any bigger, it'd hit me in the face."

"Well, how do you know the plus sign means pregnant?" I asked, grasping for straws. She looked at me like I was an idiot and even I had to laugh at that.

"This isn't my first go-around, honey." Right. Well then...

"Friggin' Dotty. I think she planned this," I half-heartedly joked. Of course I was happy, but I was still surprised. I definitely didn't expect her to get pregnant the first time we had sex in such a long ass time. Ever since that day, we'd been very careful, and I even made sure she went and got back on the pill. But like Vaeda always says…everything happens for a reason.

"Well, I mean…I am happy. Are you happy?" I asked her, hoping that she was. She nodded her head yes, and she smiled her big, toothy grin that I loved so much.

"I am. I mean…we always wanted to give Lennon a little brother or a sister. I just didn't know it would be this soon."

"I know, but here we are. We'll make it work like we always do." I kissed her lips hard and passionately, feeling every ounce of my love for her. She was carrying my child. *My* child. She was having a baby. *Our* baby.

"We're gonna have a little mutt," I said, cupping her still flat belly with the palm of my hand, provoking her to slap me on the arm.

"Don't call her that! You'll upset her."

"Did you just say…her?" I asked, arching back to look at her.

"It's just a hunch. I think it's another girl."

"Lord, help us all if it's another girl," I said, half-jokingly. The truth is I'd always wanted a little boy to throw ball with and share a special father-son bond, but if we had a girl that'd be okay too. I loved Lennon so much even when it was hard for me to accept that Shamus was a part of her like with the singing. She's always been inexplicably drawn to music. As much as I hated to admit and accept the fact that I wasn't her biological father, it was still the truth. Her love for music had only grown more intense as the years went by. I had to accept it and support her in whatever made her happy. If music makes her happy…if that's one good trait she inherited from him…then I had to support it. She may be his blood, but she was *my* daughter.

"Am I just gonna be pregnant at all of my weddings?" Vaeda asked, setting the stick down on the bathroom counter.

"This better be your last wedding, Mutt. You're stuck with me, now."

"And I couldn't be happier," she smiled against my lips as I went in for another kiss, never able to get enough of her sweet lips.

"But that reminds me," she continued. "Have you gone and talked to Liam yet?" I sighed, dreading the conversation that I knew he and I needed to have.

"Not yet. I was gonna go after the gym today." She nodded her head, and ran her long, thin hand through my hair, a gesture to let me know that it was going to be okay.

"I think it's time. Y'all have a history together. Good and bad. If your friendship is at all salvageable, then I think it's worth it." I knew she was right. I just hated the fact that we'd drifted so far apart. He had been hurting so badly that he turned to darkness all the while my life was so...*perfect*. It didn't seem fair.

***

I decided not to text or call first, because knowing him, he wouldn't respond anyway. For all I know, he could've had my number blocked. He'd gotten rid of all social media accounts, so it's not like I even had the slightest clue on how he was doing. I knew he still lived at the same apartment, because he still drove the same beat-up car that I wouldn't have caught him dead in years ago. I took a deep breath, feeling the sweat forming at my temples, as I knocked twice hard on the door. It felt like hours before it opened, and once it did, I almost wished it hadn't. The man standing on the other side looked completely unrecognizable. He had two black eyes and his bottom lip was so swollen that it pained me to even look at him.

"Greyson...what are you doing here?" he asked, almost in a whisper. His tone was somber. He looked broken down and defeated, and my eyes instantly welled with tears, unable to believe that this was the same preppy, full of life, ball-buster of a best friend I'd known all my life.

"Can...Can I come in?" I asked. He held open the door further, allowing me into his shit-hole of an apartment. It wasn't so much dirty as it was just disastrous.

Everything was a mess, clothes strewn everywhere, beer bottles and cans piled high on the coffee table. It didn't smell foul in here like it had before, but that didn't make this place any more appealing. Honestly, I was just surprised the owners hadn't evicted him yet. The place was brand new when he moved in and he'd just…destroyed it.

"I was in the process of cleaning the place up. Sorry about the mess," he said, grabbing an armful of the cans and bottles and bringing them into the kitchen. "What brings you by?"

"I uh…I just wanted to see if you'd be the best man in my wedding." He dropped the cans and bottles into a giant garbage bag, the clinking and clonking was the only thing breaking the silence. He turned to look at me like he misheard.

"I thought you were already married? You and Vaeda…You didn't…"

"No, no. I mean yes, we did have a falling out. Things haven't always been the greatest between us. But things are better now, and we decided to renew our vows and to have the wedding we didn't get a chance to have the first time," I explained. He nodded, taking it all in.

"Why me? Don't you have any other friends?" he asked, sounding disinterested in a way.

"I have friends, sure. But they're not you. You've always been my best friend, Liam. No one could ever replace that. We grew up together."

"Yeah, well…things have changed. But if you really want me to, then I guess I could stand by ya," he replied casually, as if it were no big deal.

"I mean…you don't have to. I don't want to inconvenience you. But it'd really mean a lot to me if you did."

"I'll be there, man. I wouldn't miss it. I'm glad you two ended up together. For real." There was softness to his tone that let me know that he really meant it, and it meant a lot to me.

"Yeah. Me too," I said, scratching my head, and searching for the right words to say. But as usual, my mouth was quicker than my head.

"You need help, man. Please...let me get you some help. Vaeda has this friend, and she's an alcohol and sub…"

"No. I don't need your help, nor do I want it," he quickly cut me off. He continued straightening up the kitchen; meanwhile he pulled his t-shirt up and over his head, revealing some serious new ink all down his side and his back.

"Wow. You got inked up since I last saw you, huh?" I asked, admittedly a little surprised. Liam was always more of the preppy type, pretty low-key and chill, and never showed interest in anything that was what his lifestyle was like now.

"Ah, yeah. I like the rush more than anything. Pain of the needle sure as hell beats the pain in my heart. Goddamn it, it's hot in here. Why's the AC not running, did they shut the fucking power off again?" I hadn't noticed before now, but there hadn't been a single light turned on in the place, and it actually was pretty stuffy in here. Liam flicked the kitchen light-switch on and off several times, but with no luck. It was the middle of the day, so the light illuminated through the windows pretty well, but if he had no power…did that mean he wasn't able to pay his bills?

"Are you working right now, man?" I asked out of concern.

"I got let go about a week ago because my fuck head of a boss decided to replace me with his dipshit of a son. He's about as worthless as they come. Oh well. I'll figure somethin' out."

"Your parents…do they not help you out anymore? What about Landon?" Liam shot me a glance that had an edge to it that was sharper than razor blades, and I knew I'd struck a nerve.

"My *parents* don't talk to me. They took Landon two months ago, and I haven't seen him since."

"Shit man, have you gone to court? How can they…"

"With what leg to stand on? Huh? Look at me, Greyson. I'm a fucking mess. I live in a fucking mess. *My life* is nothing but one big fucking mess. It's just as well that he lives with them for right now. He doesn't deserve this life."

"So…change it, dude. *Do something* about it. You can't just give up on your kid. That's your son! Do you think that's what Lennon would want?" I asked, regretting the words almost as soon as I said them, but it was the truth. Maybe he needed to hear it. His eyes instantly pooled with tears, and I could tell by the look on his ravaged face that he felt what I said.

"I know. Something's gotta give, man. I can't keep living like this." He leaned back against the counter and bowed his head with shame. I felt so damn helpless…I hated seeing my friend like this. This wasn't him. This wasn't how his life was supposed to be. He wanted to be a sports broadcaster when he grew up. He talked about it all the time. I was going to play for the NFL and he was going to broadcast at my games. But I was the one who made my dreams happen…all the while I left my best friend behind to bury his feelings with drugs and booze…all by his damn self.

"I can get you help. I can loan you some money until things…"

"I said no, Greyson. I don't want your pity money, and I don't want your help. Please just…let me figure this out on my own, alright? I'll find a new job and I'll get my shit together. I'll be at your wedding. But please…just leave it alone." I didn't want to leave it alone. I wanted to drag him by his ankles and throw his ass into rehab. I wanted to yell at him. To ask him how the fuck he could let his life go to such shit. Ask him how he could just let his son go like that, without even trying?! But I knew I couldn't. Because if I did, I'd be doing more damage than good, and I needed him to let me be on his side for right now.

I just hoped…that by the time he was ready to get help…that it wouldn't be too late.

Chapter Thirty-Seven

Vaeda

Five months later…

"So this is really it. The day I get to marry the love of my life for the second time," I said more to myself than to Calista, who was fanning out my dress while I looked at myself in the mirror.

"Just consider it as your fresh start," she said, smiling at me, until her face scrunched up like she were eatin' somethin' sour.

"What's wrong?" I asked, immediately in full panic mode.

"Your dress…it just feels damp right here and it smells like…did you pump gas in this thing?"

"No, it's probably just from the rain." It was pourin' outside and had been for days. The weather was sure as hell not on my side today.

"Well…you know what they say. Rain on your wedding day is good luck," she said with a reassuring smile.

"I hope so."

Calista was so damn beautiful now and all grown up. I hadn't seen her months as she's been off at college, having the time of her life. Dotty's passing was hard on her too, so I was glad that she came back to Gator Hill at all.

"I may be bias because you're my big sister, but you seriously are the prettiest bride I've ever seen." Her comment brought tears to my eyes, and I swore I wouldn't ruin my makeup for the fourth time. Stupid hormones.

"Thank you for coming back to be my bridesmaid. I know it wasn't easy for you to come back here after everything…"

"I wouldn't miss it for the world," she said, takin' a step back to admire my presence. Lennon was always supposed to be my maid-of-honor. It killed me that she wasn't with me today, and so I didn't have a maid-of-honor in physical form, but I had a candle lit in her presence and it would be next to me the whole time with a bouquet of azaleas just for her. Calista was a bridesmaid along with Juliet and Lucy from work. Greyson had Liam and three of his teammates: Dante, Cole, and Ryan.

I smiled as I looked at my reflection in the mirror; unable to fully comprehend that this was my life. It hadn't always been a fairytale, but today I definitely felt like I was a princess ready to marry and spend the rest of my life with my prince.

I wore a loose fitting gown that fit comfortably over my baby bump and had a sweetheart neckline because I know Greyson can't resist my bare shoulders. The gown was simple yet elegant, and I felt every bit as beautiful as I knew I looked. I kept my hair down in curls with the top pinned up into a braid. Nothin' too fancy, because that's just not how I am, but yet, it was just enough. I wore my mother's diamond necklace and a pair of Dotty's pearl earrings to complete my look. I really felt like they were here with me at this moment as I grasped the necklace in my hand and turned over the diamond pendant in my fingers. I closed my eyes for a second, savoring this moment in my mind.

"They'd be really proud of you, Vaeda. I know I am," Calista said gently, readin' my thoughts.

"I know. I just wish they could be here," I confessed, smiling sadly.

We were gettin' married at the church down the road from where we grew up, and we would have a small reception to follow at Uncle Henry's ranch. I didn't want a big, showy wedding with hundreds of guests I didn't even know the names of. We'd done our best to keep the wedding a secret from any outsiders, because the *last* thing either of us wanted was the press involved, especially after Greyson's pregnancy scandal. The media would eat that shit right up, and I wasn't about to have anythin' or anyone ruin our special day for us.

"Hey guys…" Juliet said as she walked in beside Lucy, and immediately covered her mouth with both of her hands. "Oh my…you look…Vaeda, you look stunning."

"Thank you. How long do we have?" I asked, hatin' to be the center of attention, even on my own wedding day.

"Like five minutes. It's already starting." My heart picked up speed so fast that I thought I was gonna faint. I took a deep breath in until my lungs started to burn, and I exhaled through my mouth, the way Dotty taught me when I was in labor.

"Let's do this thing and get our girl married! Again that is," Calista said, makin' us all laugh.

"Thank you guys for bein' by my side. It really means a lot," I said to the girls, lookin' in awe at how pretty each of them looked in the champagne colored dresses I'd hand-picked for them.

"My…look at you," Uncle Henry said, meetin' me outside the doors to link arms. He'd lost a great deal of weight in the recent months since Dotty's passing, and he'd definitely aged like hell. But it meant more to me than anything for him to be here and to be the one who walked me down the aisle.

"I love you, Uncle Henry,"

"I love you, Kiddo. More than you'll ever know." I knew he meant it.

Chapter Thirty-Eight

Greyson

Present day

My heart was using my chest as a punching bag, and I'm pretty sure I had a massive layer of sweat under this thick ass suit. My hands were jittery from the nerves, and I had to pee. Again. But it was go-time. The ceremony was about to start and every guest who mattered the most was here. Liam stood by my side, and even showed up early and at least appeared to be sober. He cleaned up well, and I was glad to have him as my best man, even if it'd been a bumpy road to get where we are.

I swear I stopped breathing the second I saw her white, flowing gown round the corner. Her eyes met mine and time fucking stopped. Blue on blue. Ice on water. Her presence, though still far away, felt thick and heavy in the air, our connection and chemistry speaking volumes through our intense gaze. That was until my vision blurred from the tears stinging my eyes, and I had to wipe them away with the back of my hand. Damn it. I swore to myself I wouldn't cry. Leave it to the Mutt to make me all soft and shit.

With every step she took, she somehow got more and more beautiful, and her familiar peach and vanilla scent assaulted my senses. I swear she must have done that on purpose. And...*her dress was strapless.* She knew how much I melted every time at the sight of her bare shoulders. I don't know what the hell it was about them, but just the site of her defined collarbone and her silky bronzed skin stirred something within me, and...yep, there it is. A fucking hard-on. Thank God the photographer we'd hired was busy snapping pictures of her and not me.

When Vaeda finally joined me at the altar, she gave her uncle a kiss on the cheek, and he took a seat in the front row next to my parents. His eyes, like mine, were brimmed with tears, and I knew it wasn't easy for him to give away the little girl he'd raised for most of her life.

"I love you," I whispered to her, meaning every word more than ever before. The feeling was so intense; I don't think I could describe it if I'd wanted to. It was the greatest feeling in the world knowing I was going to get to spend the rest of my life with my best friend. I mean, what more could I even ask for?

"I love you more," she whispered back.

"I love you the most," I teased, though I meant every word. She burst out in laughter through her own tears, and I couldn't help but embrace the cheesy, corny, goofy side that she'd opened up within me. Gone was the hard-ass, stubborn, and oftentimes selfish prick that I once was. Here was the man who was promising to be nothing but good and loving and understanding through sickness and in health…till death do us part. That's exactly what I'd promised to do. Never in my twenty-eight years of life have I ever been more sure about *anything* than I was about loving and marrying Vaeda Mutt Clarke. Tucker now. Yeah, that's right, she was actually taking my last name this time, and I made damn sure of it. She was *mine* and I wanted every dipshit and their brother to know it.

313

The minister did his thing and we lit candles for all those we'd lost along the way, and when it was finally time to kiss my bride, I swept her up into my arms, and her lips melted into mine, pressing so damn hard I almost needed my front teeth replaced. We kissed…and we kissed…and we kissed…and then out of the corner of my eye, I noticed a flicker of light. Orange. I pulled away and set her on the ground as I realized everyone was screaming…but not for us. They weren't cheering for us. They were screaming for their own damn lives because the church was suddenly on fire, and Vaeda's gown was up in flames in a split second.

"Greyson! What do I do?!" she yelled, in a state of pure panic. Without even thinking about it, I yanked my suit jacket off and wrapped it around her as best as I could. But a flame caught my arm at the same time that someone tripped over me while running the hell out.

"Greyson!" she yelled, realizing I was on the ground. It was like a fucking movie where one second everything was fine and happy, and the next second the entire room was up in flames.

"Come on, Vaeda we have to get out!" Juliet yelled, reaching her arm out to her, before I saw Liam grab her and throw her over his shoulder before running out of the church.

"I'll be back for you, man!" Liam shouted over his shoulder to me.

"No! Just run! Don't worry about me!"

"Vaeda! Run! Go…I'll be fine!" I shouted, struggling to stop the intense burn ripping through my arm and now my chest. I rolled around on the ground, breathing in nothing but fucking smoke. I coughed, my lungs rejecting the pungent smell just as I ripped open my white button down shirt to get these flames the hell off of me. I went to stand up, when it felt like a house had fallen on me. *What the hell?* I turned my head to the side to see what it was, and saw a leather dress shoe much like my own, firmly holding me in place. My eyes trailed up the black pant-leg and up to the face I hoped I'd never see again.

"Hello, Son." Surely I had to be dreaming. There was no fucking way. He was dead. He was gone. Was I in hell? Was this my punishment for everything I'd put Vaeda through?

"No," I murmured, gasping for air as his leg held more weight on me, making me struggle to breathe.

"You're dead. This isn't real," I said, feeling as if I may pass out at any given moment. Almost hoping I would.

"Oh, but I am very much alive, Son. Haven't you missed me?"

"What do you want?" I asked, feeling desperate. "Please…I'll do anything." A deep cackling laugh escaped him and he released even more weight onto my back and began kicking me in the ribs until I swear they were shattered. Kick after kick after kick. He got down onto one knee, as I gasped for air, but it hurt too much to breathe.

"Please!" I shouted. He grabbed ahold of my neck with both hands and squeezed.

"It shoulda never came down to this. You're a Davis. You betrayed our name, you cowardice sonofabitch!" he bit, his mouth foaming. He looked like a raging lunatic, and I was still flabbergasted by what was happening. This was my wedding day. My fresh start. He was supposed to be dead. Why the hell did it matter to him who the hell I married?!

"St-op. Pl-ea-se," I mouthed with what little amount of breath I had. I saw Vaeda come up from behind him out of the corner of my eye, but I didn't want to make eye contact, so as not to give him a heads up. She took her shoe off from her left foot, jerked her arm back, and smacked him hard in the head with it, the high-heel instantly gashing the side of his head, causing blood to pool down his face.

"You fucking bitch!" he roared, finally easing his grip on my neck. But the smoke was beginning to be too much. My lungs had no relief. I coughed hard and aggressively, my lungs desperate and fighting for fresh air.

"Greyson!" Vaeda screamed, her voice piercing through my ears.

"Get her out of here!" I shouted to Liam who'd run back in the building right beside Henry, who yanked her by the arm and trailed off with her. Sirens sounded in the distance, and I silently prayed they would hurry the hell up. How did this get to be my life? Why did my own father…my own flesh and fucking blood…hate me so goddamn much?

"Who the hell are you?!" my father shouted at Colt, positioning himself chest-to-chest with him.

"Dad, no! I'll be okay, just get the hell out of here! Where's Mom?" I asked, realizing I hadn't seen her leave with everyone else. Colt eyed my father up and down, looking intrigued that anyone was stepping up to him. As far as I knew, no one ever had.

"I'm the one my son should've warned you about. I'm the most feared man in the goddamn south. I'm about to put a bullet through your son's goddamn skull. Should I do you first? Or do you wanna watch?" Colt asked, pointing the gun he'd pulled out from his holster to my father's head and then to mine.

"You really have the fucking balls to call him your son? What kind of father do you think you are?" my dad asked, his mouth foaming with the heat of his words, not backing down for one second.

"I'm the kind of father who's loyal to his goddamn name. I'm a Davis, motherfucker," Colt spewed, puffing

318

his chest up to my father, and holding the gun under his chin.

"If I pull the trigger right here, it'll blast through the top of your head. But if I blast it through your fucking mouth…" he maneuvered the gun so quickly into my father's mouth, I didn't even see it coming. "Then it'll go through the back. What would look nicer for your funeral? Oh wait…they probably wouldn't do an open casket. On second thought…they might not have a funeral for you at all. Besides…your wife could care less about you. She was fucking another man behind your back after all…wasn't she?" My father's eyes were wide and frantic, not knowing if he should speak, move, or just hold still. I wanted to do something, anything to help him. But if I was too slow or if I made the wrong move, he could pull the trigger and my father would be dead. *Think Greyson, fucking think! Think! You're running out of time!* I could barely see through the thick wave of black smoke, but I heard the firemen enter the building, shouting to anyone who may be in here.

"Don't. Fucking. Speak," Colt gritted at me through his teeth. If I yelled for help, he'd blow my father's head off. But if I didn't yell for help…we might all burn to the ground.

"Do you think your wife is taken care of by now?" Colt asked, cocking his head to the sky like he was lost in thought. "Probably. It doesn't take that long. Say hello to her for me, will ya?" he said, cocking his gun back, ready to shoot.

"NO!!!!" I shouted, just as the blast of the bullet rang through my ears. It was a sound I would never be able to get out of my fucking head. A sound that would haunt me forever.

"Dad!" I screamed, my eyes burning, unable to see where he'd fallen.

"God, I've waited a long fucking time to do that," an unfamiliar yet familiar voice said, from behind me. Next thing I knew I was being carried out of the burning church, and everything went black.

***

I woke up to a crowd of people hovered around me, but the first person I saw was my wife. Thank God.

"Vaeda…" I murmured, causing me to cough more, but it hurt like hell to do it. Everything hurt. "Where's Lennon?" I asked.

"She's okay, your mom has her. She took her to the ranch. She didn't see anything."

"My mom…she's okay?" I asked, remembering what Colt had said. She nodded her head, with tears streaming down her pretty little made-up face.

"She's okay, Greyson."

"Colt? Where is he…I'll…I'll fucking…kill…him," I bit out, struggling to talk. My lungs hurt too much. My ribs.

"Already taken care of, Brother." I turned my head to the right, and saw Drifter Davis was standing over me, covered in blood and smoke. I opened my mouth to speak…to try and make sense of it all…but Vaeda shhh'd me with her delicate finger to my lips.

"Shhh, Greyson. It's all over now. It's gonna be okay. Drifter came here with Colt, but not for the reasons you think. He was instructed to take your mom out and then me, and Colt was going to deal with your dad and you. *My dad. Where is my dad?*

"But Drifter didn't harm your mother. He made sure she got out safely with Lennon. He shot and killed Colt, Greyson. He saved all of our lives," Vaeda said, smiling through her tears up at Drifter.

"He's really gone. For good this time," she confirmed.

"Colt wanted to fake his own death. He was being hunted every which way for Sunday from every club all the way up to New York City. It was only a matter of time before he was killed. But I wanted to do the honors," Drifter admitted.

"You…shoulda…let…me…do it." Drifter shook his head at me.

"Nah, man. You don't want that on your shoulders. Trust me. I'm already going to Hell for the things I've done. You…you're good. You have a family. A life. You don't need anything weighing you down or keeping you up at night."

"Tyson Davis…You have a warrant out for your arrest. Anything you say can and will be held against you in a court of law. If you cannot afford an attorney, one will be appointed to you…" a tall, stocky officer said, approaching Drifter.

"Yeah, yeah, I know the drill," he said, placing his hands into a surrendering gesture and then holding them behind his back so they could cuff him.

"I'm sorry for everything, Brother," he said over his shoulder as the officer and his partner dragged him away.

"Thank you," I mouthed to him, unable to speak. Paramedics surrounded me, lifting me up onto a gurney.

"It's okay, baby. I'll be right there with you the whole time," Vaeda said, walking alongside the two men who carried me into the ambulance. They gave me some meds that knocked me on my ass and I didn't remember anything until I got to the hospital.

When we got to the hospital, I was immediately assessed and had needles poking and prodding me, tubes sticking out every which way, and monitors surrounding me. I was placed on oxygen for the smoke inhalation, and told that I was lucky as hell that I was alive and without serious damage to my lungs, although it felt awful. They ran tests and x-rays, and the only injury I incurred was four broken ribs, which would heal on their own with time. I had second-degree burns on my arm and chest, but it wasn't nearly as bad as it could've been.

Vaeda was seated to my right, clutching tightly to my hand. I turned my head slowly and saw my father standing in front of me…looking unharmed, but scared as hell.

"I'm okay. I'm not hurt," he said, by way of explanation as soon as I opened my mouth to speak. "I wanted to be here when you were more with it, but I need to go and fill your mother in and make sure she and Lennon are holding up alright." I nodded, tears welling up in my eyes, feeling extremely thankful that he was still here with us. He wasn't shot. Colt was shot. Colt was dead. *Really* dead this time.

I'm sorry, Vaeda…I know how much this wedding meant to you," I rasped.

"You can always have a third wedding," Liam said, seated to the left of me. I was surprised to see him here, but also so very glad that he was.

"No," Vaeda shook her head and chuckled. "No more weddings for me."

After the doctor came back in to check on me again, Liam stood up from his seat, and reached into his pants pocket.

"I uh…I found this after Lennon died. It was a letter she'd written for your wedding. A maid of honor speech, I guess. I saved it and planned to give it to you one day," he said to Vaeda. "I was going to read it at the reception, but well…here it goes." He unfolded the piece of paper with trembling hands, and he sniffled and cleared his throat.

Vaeda,

I hope that this letter finds its way into your hands one day. I probably won't be around to read it to you in person, but just know that I am so incredibly proud of you. I know I was always supposed to be your maid of honor, and I am so sorry that I can't physically be there with you, but just know I am always with you in whatever way I can be. If I know you at all, I know you're marrying the love of your life, Greyson Tucker. You may not know it at the time that I'm currently writing this...but you'll figure it out eventually. You love him, Vaeda, and he loves you. You two will end up together, and I'll be cheering you on from wherever I am. So here it goes...

Vaeda and Greyson sittin' in a tree...no I'm totally kidding.

Vaeda and Greyson,

I can feel it deep in my bones that you two will end up together. It may not always be easy. Love never is. Your love may not have come as easily as mine has with Liam. And that's okay. That was our love story, and this is yours. It doesn't make it any less real. I've been lucky enough to be able to witness your love story. The good and the bad. Vaeda, I know you don't see the way Greyson looks at you like you're the only one in the room and just stares right through you when he thinks no one is watching. And Greyson, I know you don't think that she's good enough for you, but only someone who's been on the outside looking in can see the real truth. You two belong together. I know it and you know it. I wish you nothing but a lifetime of complete and true happiness. I love you both so much. Yes, even you Greyson, even though you made me fall off the monkey bars. I'm leaving you with a big responsibility. I need you to take care of my girl. She's stronger than hell, but she'll need you to be her arms of comfort when I can't be.

XOXO,

Love Always,

Lennon James

None of us spoke a word. The silence sent a ringing through my ears after he was finished reading. Liam had obviously already read the letter, and I could see the pain etched onto his face. He ran his thumb back and forth over the paper and held it up to his lips. He turned and handed the piece of paper out to Vaeda, and walked out of the room, probably to gather his thoughts and get some fresh air. Vaeda's eyes were blurred with tears, although I think they'd been like that for most of the day.

"That was somethin' huh?" she spoke in a soft whisper. I nodded my head, not knowing what to say. Lennon always did have a way with words.

"I think she was with all of us today. What do you think?" It was Vaeda's turn to nod her head in agreement.

"I know she was. I talked to Drifter before they brought you out…Calista thought she smelled gasoline on my dress where there was a wet spot near the bottom when I put it on, but there was no stain, so I just brushed it off because the only place my dress had been was my closet and then the church. I figured maybe it was condensation from my water bottle or something. Turns out Colt had gotten ahold of the dress before I arrived this morning and he dumped lighter fluid along the bottom. He knew we were lighting a candle for Lennon down by my side. He had this all planned out, Greyson. He knew my dress would catch on fire. He knew everything' about the wedding, and the media knew too. They were all over outside until your dad and Uncle Henry threatened them if they didn't leave. So if the media knew…that means someone on the inside had leaked information about the wedding."

I didn't have to guess who it fucking was.

"I'm feeling a little tired and overwhelmed, baby. Do you think you could just give me a few minutes? I know you must be exhausted and overwhelmed too…"

"Of course. I'll go back and check on Lennon and everyone else. Calista's waiting outside for me in the waiting room. I'll come back later, okay? Call if you need anything." And with that, she kissed me on the cheek and was out the door. I sighed heavily, and ran my hand through my hair wondering where the fuck to go from here. But what I heard next…told me everything I needed to know.

"Yes, I'm sure. You guys have already done enough. No, damn it! I said I needed the money by today, not tomorrow, not Monday, *today*. I'm not telling you one more goddamn thing! I'll come and pick up the money in a little while. Goodbye." Liam hung up his cell phone and stuffed it into his slacks pocket, before coming back into the room.

"Did Vaeda head out?" he asked, seeming nonchalant.

"Yeah. I wanted us to be alone when I break your fucking jaw. You better tell them to get another bed ready because you're about to be in worse shape than I am, *friend.*" I growled, sitting up further in the bed, contemplating jumping up and ripping these fucking wires out.

"Whoa, man. Calm down…"

"Shut the fuck up and sit down," I demanded, giving him one chance to explain himself, and one chance only. He did as I said, but he looked uncomfortable while his hands fidgeted in his lap and the sweat pooled at his temples and upper lip.

"Who were you just on the phone with?" I asked, already knowing the answer. This was a test.

"My um…uh…"

"Think very carefully before you lie to me, Liam."

"Man, I'm sorry. I'm so fucking sorry. I needed the money and…"

"Are you high right now?" I asked, cocking my head to the side. He was slurring his speech and his pupils were insanely dilated. He didn't answer, he just looked straight at me until the guilt set in, and he was no longer able to look into my eyes. He bowed his head and I heard a sob catch in the back of his throat. He nodded twice, and placed his elbows onto his knees, his hands together into a prayer gesture.

"I need help, Greyson. I do. I need help, man." The words I'd waited so damn long to hear cut me right to my core. I'd so desperately wanted him to come to me for help, but having him actually do it made it all the more real. My best friend was an alcoholic and a drug addict. He needed my help.

"I know you guys didn't want the media involved…but I needed the money really badly. I'm almost completely out of my shit…and I needed to get more. I thought I could just stop. I thought I wasn't addicted, and just wanted the drugs…not needed them." The tears poured down his face, each one faster than the one before it. My heart fucking broke for him. I was pissed as hell that he'd lied to me. He got the media involved, and therefore, put my entire family and myself in danger. I tried not to be mad at him. I swear I did. I tried to remember that everything happens for a reason. If he didn't leak the wedding to the media then Colt wouldn't have shown up and wouldn't be dead right now. Really dead. I tried to tell myself if he didn't come after me today, he surely would have tried another time. But Liam betrayed me. My best fucking friend who I'd bent over backwards for time and time again…trying to help him…trying to be his friend…*and he betrayed me.*

"I will get you the help you need. You won't need to worry about a thing. But after I do…I want you to get the fuck out of my life," I said, causing his head to jerk back by what I'd said. He nodded his understanding, his lips pursed tightly together.

"I understand…I'm really sorry, Greyson. So fucking sorry." I knew he was. But I didn't have room in my life for half-ass people anymore. Not everyone you meet in life is meant to be there permanently, and unfortunately for me, it seemed that was most of the people in my life. I had a wife, a daughter, and a baby on the way to worry about now. I needed to be present for *them*. They were my permanent people. My forever.

Chapter Thirty-Nine

Vaeda

Three years later…

Today is the biggest day of the year for our family. It was Superbowl Sunday, and the most exciting one yet. The Tennessee Titans were playin' against the Cowboys. I was so extremely proud of Greyson for leadin' the team this far and makin' all of his dreams come true. His excitement was contagious and all four of us had butterflies in our belly. Yes, four. Though it was soon to be six. Yep, you heard that right. Greyson and I welcomed a little boy named Levi, two years ago, and any day now, we were addin' two more to our crazy little family. *Twins.* Bein' an only child, I always knew I wanted a house full of kids, and the fact that it was becoming my reality was truly amazing. More than I could've ever asked for. We didn't know the sex of the twins, we wanted it to be a surprise, but deep down I secretly hoped for one of each. If not, we'd just have to try again to try and even out the score. Greyson was such an incredible dad even with his busy schedule, and I couldn't have asked for a better partner to go through life with. I can honestly say that for the first time in my life, I was truly nothing but just plain…*happy*.

Greyson continued to travel back and forth between Gator Hill and Nashville for a while after we got married, but as more time passed by, I realized Gator Hill just didn't feel like my home anymore. Ever since…the wedding when everything changed. Dotty wasn't there anymore to make it feel like home, and the rest of us were just tryin' our best to move forward and heal from everything that happened. I think Gator Hill would've just held us back from that. Greyson and I both attended therapy regularly to talk about our feelings about the events that transpired on our wedding day. The day that was supposed to be so special to us and be the happiest day of our lives was just a bad memory I wanted to forget. It was a little difficult at first to adjust to life in Nashville, but I quickly found out that I fit in perfectly when I accepted a position as a

surgical resident at the Vanderbilt University Medical
Center. As it turns out, we weren't totally alone, because
Greyson put Liam up in a rehab here in Nashville, so he
could be closer to him and keep an eye on him. After he got
out, he decided to stay, and he and Juliet who were now
together, lived right next door to us. It wasn't an easy road
to get him sober, or to accept that he deserved happiness as
much as the rest of us. But you'll hear all about that another
time.

Our son Levi was now two, and Lennon was the
absolute best big sister, despite her callin' him The
Cockblocker because she overheard her father callin' him
that one night. We tried to explain to her that it wasn't a
very nice word, but she was almost twelve years old goin'
on twenty, and the sass and hormones flowin' through her
was just too much to argue with sometimes.

"MOOOOMMMMM! The Cockblocker won't stop
tryin' to mess with my guitar, and I'm trying to sing!"
Lennon shouted in her overdramatic twang-filled voice.
Lennon has been singin' and practicing the guitar for years,
and she was a natural. She sang country, of course, and the

337

mere sound of her melody gave me chill bumps every time she sang. I swear she sang more than she talked. As soon as she got home from school, she would toss her backpack in the mudroom, and run up the stairs and pick up her guitar. I had to pound on her locked door more often than not to come out for supper and to do her homework. It's like she was one with the music, and her guitar was an extension of her body. I loved that she found somethin' she was so passionate about, and as a mother, I would always support her dreams, even if it killed me a little inside.

***

"How's everyone doin' tonight?!" the familiar voice blasted through the speakers, as I watched his body from the VIP stands, lookin' so small in the center of thousands of people who were cheerin' him on. "SHAY! SHAY! SHAY!"

"WE LOVE YOU, HEARTTHROB!!!" a female voice rang loudly through the crowd. I took a deep breath and hoped that I'd made the right decision. She didn't know her true identity, but it was only a matter of time. Greyson and I had talked about it, and although we knew it would eventually be in her best interest to know the truth…it didn't make it hurt any less. We didn't want her to grow up hating us for keepin' her from her biological father, and I felt it in my heart that this was a step in the right direction for her. But was it best for me? I was in full panic-mode, knowin' that my daughter was about to meet him for the very first time on national live television.

"I know this wasn't planned and I'll probably get my ass sued for this…shit, sorry I just swore didn't I? Damn, I did it again," he stammered, and I could tell he was just as nervous as I was, even though the crowd went wild with laughter. In their eyes, Shay Tucker could do no wrong. No matter how many times he'd messed up or how much time he'd served, bein' away from his music, each time he sang, it was like he'd never stopped. He'd broken records left and right, and he didn't even have to try. Like Lennon, it just came natural to him. A gift that they both had and shared. It was what brought them together, yet separated them from the rest of us.

"I'd like to bring out my very talented niece to join me in singin' the National Anthem for y'all tonight. She's got music in her blood and I couldn't be more proud of the talent she has and the star I know she'll be one day. Everybody put your hands up for LENNON TUCKERRRR!" he shouted, makin' my heart accelerate to maximum speed. Despite the confused looks on many faces, the crowd once again went crazy and they started cheerin' her on too.

"LENN-ON! LENN-ON! LENN-ON!" It was such a bizarre experience, and as soon as her tiny little frame ran out and stood right next to him, it was as though she'd belonged there the entire time. She didn't appear the least bit nervous, but rather like she'd been doin' this her whole life.

With a single head-nod from Shamus, the music started playin' and their voices floated through the air, in perfect synchrony like they'd practiced this a thousand times. Except they hadn't, and they'd never sang together before. Never even stood next to each other. And yet, here they were singin' the National Anthem at the Superbowl. Their voices were one with each other, and they sang in perfect synchrony, both of their voices so powerful, even on their own, and both of them together brought on a powerhouse of emotions that ran through me. It was so beautiful, so intense, and so overwhelming all at once. I wish I could see Greyson's face right now, but I knew he could feel it too.

When they were finished, the clapping and the chanting was so deafening and vibrated right through me. Lennon jumped right into his arms, and he spun her around into a full circle like she weighed nothin' at all, before setting her back down and planting' a kiss to the top of her head.

"I'm so dang proud of you, you know that?" I told Lennon as I watched her eyes light up like it was Christmas morning.

"I know," she said with a smile, before lookin' up at me thoughtfully. "I know you and Daddy haven't always gotten along with Uncle Shamus, but he's really nice,

Mama. He's so cool! Can we have him over for dinner sometime? Plllleeeeeease?!" she pleaded, placin' her hands at her chest into a prayer gesture. My heart fell into the pit of my stomach, wishing we weren't having this conversation right now, but knowing all along that one day we would.

"I'll talk to Daddy about it, okay?" I promised.

***

The Titans took home their Superbowl win with a score of 31-20. Greyson and his teammates played their hearts out, and it was so much fun to watch, even while chasin' around a two year old in the VIP room.

It was the middle of the night by the time we were on our way home after interviews, and making a quick appearance at the after party, and we were all exhausted. My eyes were heavy, and my body was cramping up from the long, restless day.

"Ugh, I think the twins are as worn out as I am, they're punishin' me now for not gettin' any rest," I said, arching my back and rubbin' my sore belly. One of them must have been right under my ribs in the most God-awful position because uncomfortable was by far an understatement.

"Oh, Mamaaaa. The Mutts are comin' ouuuttaaaaa ya. They say it's your karmaaaa. For not layin' downaaaa," Lennon sang from the backseat, guitar in hand. Greyson and I looked at each other and busted out in laughter at her made-up lyrics and her use of her father's nickname for the babies and me.

"Oh no. Mama's not goin' into labor until she gets some sleep."

But just then, as if right on cue, my mid-section felt like a chainsaw had ripped right through me, tearing through my insides. My breathing hitched, and my legs tensed up. Sweat was pooling at my temples, and my heart was in the back of my throat. These babies weren't startin' things off slowly that's for sure, because that was a full-blown dang contraction that quite literally took my breath away.

"Are you alright?" Greyson asked nervously from the driver's seat.

"Yeah. I'm okay. Just uncomfortable," I lied through my damn teeth. I didn't want to admit it, but these babies were comin' out whether I was rested up and ready or not.

"Here, drink some water," he offered, handin' me the three-day-old Dasani bottle from the cup holder between us.

"I think I'll pass," I scoffed, rolling my eyes at him.

"Ohhh, Mamaaaa. The Mutts are comin' ouuuuttaaaa."

"No! Damn it, I'm not in labor!" I shouted, instantly feeling bad for yellin' at her.

"Are ya sure about that?" Greyson asked, looking at the growing wet spot that quickly turned into a puddle between my legs. *SHIT.*

Epilogue

Greyson

Six months later...

I never thought it was possible to hold so much goddamn love in my heart. I never thought I'd be able to divide my love in so many ways, but here I was...so completely and irrevocably head-over-heels in love with five people: My wife, my two daughters, and my two sons. My heart has officially swelled beyond maximum capacity, as the tears streamed one right after another down my proud ass face as I looked at my wife. *My beautiful, selfless, incredible goddamn wife.* The one I thought I would never give the time of day. The one who got on every last nerve I had and then somehow managed to find one more. The one who has had so much patience with me...sometimes more than I deserved.

If there's one thing I can tell you, it's that our love did not come easy. It was hard. It was painful. It was sacrifice and compromise, and it was…anything but beautiful at times. But somehow through it all, through all the loss, the arguments, the betrayals, and the games…we both grew up. We had to do it on our own. We had to lose ourselves, and each other, to find ourselves again. In the end, I think that's what made us stronger. I had to learn to accept that blood does not define love, and blood does not define who I was as a person. Colt Davis…he may have given me my DNA…but I never would be anything like him. *I am in control of my own goddamn destiny. My rage does not define me. I am a good person, and an excellent husband. I am one badass motherfucking father.*

As I sat there with my beer in hand, and a smile on my face, I looked around the table at all the people I loved the most. I found myself thanking God for bringing us all back together again. I couldn't help but feel deep in my bones that Dotty had a little something to do with it. She did bring Vaeda and I back together after all.

"Uncle Shamus will you sing with me?" Lennon asked from across the table. His face instantly lit up and then fell, realizing that there may be some hard feelings.

"Go ahead," I said with a nod in his direction, letting him know that it was okay. "But after…we all need to talk." Our eyes met and my bottom lip trembled with what I was about to do, bit was time. Vaeda's eyes glossed over with fresh tears as she nodded her consent.

"Wait!" Juliet shouted from her spot at the table. "I want to make a toast to Liam before y'all run off. Today marks two years of sobriety for the greatest man I've gotten the pleasure to know. And honey, I am so, so proud of you and all of your hard work," she said, looking longingly into his eyes as we all clapped and cheered for him.

"Thank you. I owe it all to this couple sitting right here," he said, referring to Vaeda and I. "Y'all gave me hope and the means for a better life when I didn't have a pot to piss in. It's because of you that I'm where I'm at today. Thank you…for never giving up on me, even when I so desperately wanted to give up on myself." His eyes were full of tears and gratitude. Yet there was something else, something I couldn't quite put my finger on.

"But there's one more thing," he added, and the silence in the room was deafening. The anticipation of what he was about to say nearly killed me. Nobody moved or said a word. We all just waited…none of us expecting what was going to happen next.

"Juliet and I are getting married." My muscles relaxed, and my face softened. I swore, I thought it was going to be something bigger than that. "And with Lennon's blessing, she's officially adopting Landon." My jaw. Hit. The. Fucking. Floor.

The End

For Vaeda and Greyson.
Stayed tuned for Liam's story
coming soon...

About the Author

Alexis Bice is an indie author from Upstate New York. As a mother of two little ones, time to write never comes easy, but whether it's just a few minutes or sentences each day, she makes it happen. Alexis says that books are an extension of her body. She is constantly reading and learning new things and doing extensive research for her books. It is her escape from reality, if only for a short while.

To stay up to date on all things book related, follow:

Instagram: alexis_bice_author

Facebook: Alexis Bice Author

Website: authoralexisbice.com

Thank you so much for reading! I hope you enjoyed this book as much as I enjoyed writing it. **Please consider leaving an honest review on amazon to help me out!** I appreciate YOU so very much!